DRAGON'S INSTINCT

A DAY CARE FOR SHIFTERS

ELVA BIRCH

For Kayti.
The blueberries are your fault.

CHAPTER 1

Shots sizzled across the speeder's bow and Turnkey dove at the controls. "We've got a problem!" he hollered back to the engineer.

"You're telling me!" Tagrin shouted back. "We've got a coolant leak in the quarterdeck and a crack in the second hull! She's not going to hold together long enough to break atmo!"

"I know how to fix this!" Turnkey said—

Ian stopped typing, his fingers poised over the laptop.

He had no *idea* how to fix this.

It had taken him twenty minutes to re-read and remember where he was even going with his plot when he sat down to write and his brain felt shattered. He couldn't recall when he'd last gotten a full night's sleep or more than an hour of writing time in one sitting. Every time that he so much as started feeling like he was making progress on his book, his toddler daughter, Lucy, needed a snack, or a new diaper, or a hug, or a nap, or it was time for a meal or to do laundry or there was a toy that needed to be repaired.

Or, like now, there was suspicious silence, which was even worse.

Ian thought he'd have a little window of writing opportunity. Lucy had been happily playing with her food at the table, and as slow as she ate, Ian guessed he might be able to get a few hundred words written.

He didn't want to think about how a few hundred words at a time wasn't going to get him finished by the publisher's (third) deadline, or how many times he'd had to delete big chunks because he was incapable of holding the whole book in his head and his plot had gone straight off the tracks.

"Lu?"

Ian leaned back in his chair so that he could see into the kitchen.

Lucy's chair was empty, and her purple butterfly dress was hanging off the back of it. It hung neatly, as if she had taken it off before she shifted.

Ian swore under his breath and cheerfully called, "Lucy? Honey? Did you finish your food?" He should have kept her in a high chair a little longer, he thought woefully. But she was tall for her age and had convinced him that she was ready for a big girl chair. She was, but was he?

The sandwich that she'd been playing with had been disassembled and all the parts she liked had been eaten out. The halved cherry tomatoes were gone, of course, they never lasted long enough to be entertainment. Her sippy cup was on its side, a few drops of water on the table beneath it.

"Lucy, you know I don't want to play hide and seek right now. Lucy?"

Ian was equal parts annoyed and worried. There was so much trouble that a little girl could get into...and even more that a squirrel could. She'd been so safely occupied, and he'd barely looked away. He was the worst dad, he was a miserable failure, how hard could it be to juggle a stay-at-home career and one small child?

Pretty damned hard, it turned out. Ian scanned the top of the fridge and the cabinets in the kitchen; Lucy liked high places. But she wasn't in any of her usual spots, and Ian spread his search zone down the hall. "Lucy, please come out. Honey, are we playing a game? You know that Daddy needs to get his book finished, but if you want me to, I can read you one of *your* books. Lucy?"

The carpet gave a suspicious squelch, right in front of the bathroom and Ian flung the door open to find that there was water in a shallow pool all across the floor. "Argh!" He was wearing socks, and they were immediately soaked as he dashed across to the sink, where the tap was still running. There was a washcloth lying across the bottom of the bowl and when Ian pulled it out, the water in the bowl swiftly drained away. A few water-logged dolls sagged at the bottom.

"Lucy!!"

Ian made himself temper his voice. Lucy had probably realized that she'd done something wrong and was hiding as a squirrel in one of the million tiny places in this house where he'd never find her.

"Lucy, you aren't in trouble," he called as gently as he could. "I just need to know that you're okay!"

He pulled the towels down off the rack to start sopping up the puddle. He had a box fan somewhere, he'd better get it going in the hallway before they had a mold problem to add to the mix.

The phone rang while he was wringing out the towels for the second time. "Hang on," he said when the fan drowned out the caller.

"You sound like you're in an air tunnel," Wanda

complained when he got the fan turned off. When Ian was feeling his most lonely and full of regret over their broken relationship, she usually managed to say just the right thing to remind him why they'd parted ways.

"Sorry," he said, knowing he didn't sound sorry. "What's up?"

"I wanted to talk about The Schedule."

She always said it like both words were capitalized.

The Schedule.

The Schedule was the calendar that dictated the days they had to see each other, the days that Lucy was hers or his. At first, Wanda had been adamant about getting every day allotted to her with their joint custody, and Ian had spent the days she was gone desperately missing his daughter. But Wanda got busier with work, her new boyfriend had kids, and Wanda had gradually adjusted The Schedule so that Ian had Lucy nearly all the time. He'd even thought about pressuring her for child support, but it had never felt like he was equal to the effort.

"After all," she'd said more than once. "You don't work, it's not an inconvenience to you."

Ian wasn't sure which part of her assumption he objected to most. That writing wasn't working? That raising a small child basically by himself wasn't a whole job all by itself? But like most battles with Wanda, it simply wasn't worth fighting anymore.

"What about it?" Ian sounded more surly than he meant. Was she going to want to talk to Lucy? Did he have to admit that he didn't know where she was and that she'd just flooded the bathroom?

Wanda sounded almost sweet. "I know I said I didn't want any of the holidays this year, but my parents invited us up to Helena for Labor Day. They'd like to see Lucy."

Ian remembered holidays with Wanda's folks. They

were all squirrel shifters, and while he adored his daughter beyond reason, the ceaseless chattering and the way Wanda's family was always in constant motion always left him feeling like he'd been in a room full of mental vampires after only a few minutes. Having to stay with them had been a kind of fine-tuned torture.

Labor Day. "Let me check my calendar."

Ian didn't really have to look at it. Aside from the looming red BOOK DUE (really, this time!) entry on his calendar, it was just a trudging list of nothing. The closest he'd gotten to a social life lately was babysitting his friend Roderick's daughter Gabby, a little girl just younger than Lucy, while Roderick took his new girlfriend out on a date.

Sometimes, it seemed like everyone was moving on without him.

"That should work fine," Ian said.

"You're a peach," Wanda said sunnily. "I'll pick her up that Saturday morning and drop her off on Monday evening. Let me talk to Lucy."

Dammit.

"Hang on." He muted the phone, double-checking that he had, and then hollered, "Lucy! Come talk to your mom! She's on the phone *right now!*"

A rustle at the baseboard gave him a few seconds of warning, and then Lucy shot out from behind the heater, her rusty red fur covered in dust.

She flowed up into a little girl, completely naked, and reached grabby hands for the phone.

"I'll hold it for you, honey," Ian said, thumbing the connection back on. He knew there were parents that would casually hand children Lucy's age a several hundred dollar phone—Wanda among them—but he didn't trust her attention span and he couldn't afford to replace it.

"Mummy! Bathroom's all wet!"

Ian couldn't hear Wanda's answer to that, and he oversaw half of a halting conversation before Lucy agreed, "Kisses!" and waved at the phone.

Ian checked to see that Wanda had hung up and put the phone back in his pocket. "You want to tell me about the bathroom?" he asked.

Lucy eyed her escape route back under the heater and Ian made a note to try to block it up with something. His entire house had become an obstacle course of trying to keep her out of small places and dangerous things. The cabinet locks were a constant frustration, as much for him as they were for her, and she could climb *anything*.

"You're not in trouble," Ian promised. "I just want to make sure it doesn't happen again, honey."

She wilted and mumbled something about dolls, carrots, and possibly a trombone.

"Just make sure you ask me before you play in the bathroom," Ian begged. "And turn off the water. We don't want to waste it!"

Lucy looked up at him hopefully, then said, "I'm hungry."

It was her get-out-jail-free card. Ian wasn't going to deny her *food*, no matter how recently she'd eaten, and he bent and scooped her up into his arms. "What did you forget, sweety?"

Lucy put two fingers in her mouth and said, "Clothes?" around them.

"Clothes," Ian agreed. "You're supposed to take your clothes with you when you shift."

Ian found himself at eye level with the business card magnet that Roderick had given him the week before as he opened the fridge. Cherry's new day care for shifter children, Tiny Paws, apparently taught kids to shift with their clothing.

A day care for shifter children.

Maybe he could talk Wanda into helping to pay for it. Maybe, if he could finish his damned book, he could pay for it himself. It would be good for Lucy to get more socialization. He couldn't just go set up playdates with the neighborhood kids when she was so good at shifting and so terrible about knowing when she was supposed to.

"Do you want a yogurt squeezie?" Ian offered. He knew she would.

When he put her down for a protesting nap, an hour later, he went back to his laptop. There were sticky squirrel footprints on the lid.

I know how to fix this, he thought hopefully.

He opened up his phone and punched in the number for Tiny Paws.

"Hi," he said when Cherry answered. "I was wondering if you had any openings…"

CHAPTER 2

"Here we are, Seltzer," Olivia said, unlocking the front door with the key that had been left under the mat for her in a quaint, small town style. "Home, sweet, home."

Seventeen Crescent Drive wasn't much to look at.

Olivia had been expecting a posher neighborhood from the sticker shock of the lease; she'd taken the teaching contract before she went shopping for a rental and that had turned out to be a big mistake. If she hadn't wanted to leave Florida and start over so badly, she might have tried to get out of it, but maybe she could get a second job. Maybe even taking wedding photos.

Olivia paused to let the wave of grief and anger wash over her, then pulled the key out of the deadbolt. Maybe not taking photos. She stuffed those memories back and opened the door.

She could probably find temporary work as a waitress or a cashier before school started. She was walking distance to the middle school, so she could keep her commute costs down.

Seltzer, impressed by neither her life plans or their destination, meowed from the cat carrier. Olivia released the hatch on his door and the big orange cat flowed out, fluffy tail high. He sniffed around the porch and sauntered into the house, prepared to investigate every corner of his new domain.

Olivia turned before following him, gazing around outside.

The houses were close together and small, but there were a lot of trees and everything seemed bright and tidy. It was a quiet suburb, with half a dozen kids in the street enjoying the last weeks of their summer break on bikes and a few people out doing yard work in the sunshine.

There was a quality to the air that was very different than the humid air of Florida. It was more than just dry; it actually felt more friendly. Olivia didn't think it was just the mild temperature or the ideal water content, but she couldn't identify the smell it had. Trees, maybe? Was it the variety of grass on the lawns here, which looked thinner and paler than the lawns she was used to?

There were sounds of insects, if she listened for them, but it wasn't the same din that she was used to, and the blue sky was just a little hazy. There were wildfires further north, apparently a common hazard of Montana, but all of the current blazes were comfortably far from civilization. There were birds flitting around in the trees that Olivia didn't recognize, but she heard a few familiar calls.

The interior of the house was exactly as it had been in the videochat tour with her realtor, Veronica. It had a sparse, open floor plan with a living area and kitchen, a bathroom and one bedroom in the back. It was unfurnished, with old but un-stained beige carpet in most rooms, and textured white walls. The kitchen was unremarkable, with melamine counters and box store cabinets. The appliances were white, and the cabinets had a pale, worn wood finish.

Everything was perfectly serviceable and completely impersonal.

Well, Olivia was here for a year, at least, and she could make it her own. For tonight, she was roughing it on an inflatable mattress with a sleeping bag. She opened the back door and looked out at the overgrown garden. It was probably too late in the season to make much of it, being the first week of August, but maybe next summer she could grow tomatoes and peas in the raised beds. There were some volunteer sunflowers that had grown up around an empty bird feeder and a lot of weeds that Olivia wasn't familiar with.

There was an alley beyond the garden, with a wooden fence. Chain link separated her from the neighbor on one side, and wood on the other. The back yard was gated off from the front, and the fencing back here was much taller than in front. Perhaps the previous renter had a dog.

Seltzer squeezed past her with an imperious *mmmrrrrt!* and went to search the yard. Not in the least bit worried about his ability to protect himself and confident that he wouldn't go far or be away long, Olivia remembered that she had perishable groceries in the car and went to unload it.

The groceries were wedged at the top of her over-stuffed car and she managed to crush her loaf of bread getting it out. Once Olivia had put the food away in the empty cabinets and fridge, she started bringing in the boxes, heaping them along the wall of the appropriate room in tidy rows. *Books, bedding, clothes.* Every box was labeled, some of them more creatively than others: *Camera stuff, photos, bathroom things, I don't know what this is but I can't get rid of it.* Seltzer managed to find a different way to be underfoot with every trip.

She was hauling her last box in, sweaty and feeling accomplished, when she saw a man in the next yard creeping around near the low chain link fence that separated the properties. She tightened her grip, mentally cataloging the contents of the box, *knick knacks*, for handy weapons. Nickel City certainly seemed like a nice safe place, but there were weirdos everywhere.

"Hi!" she called, determined to make a brave show.

The man straightened quickly, and Olivia thought that he looked too genuinely surprised to have been stalking her. He was about her age, she thought, late twenties or early thirties. His short, sandy hair was standing up in a few places, as if he'd just been running his fingers nervously through it. He was pale, like he didn't spend much time outside, but looked fit. "Oh, hi," he said, with half a wave. "I, ah. Was looking for my daughter? She's a bit of an escape artist."

He was looking for his daughter in the tall grass at the base of the fence? He seemed nice enough, but Olivia was immediately wary.

"How old is she?" she asked. "I could...help you look?" Olivia was trying to remember where she'd left her phone in case she needed to call the cops—either to help this guy out or to report his escape from a mental institution. It was probably in her purse, on the kitchen counter with the boxes labeled *kitchen junk I probably don't need.* It had been the last box she wedged into her station wagon.

"She's nearly two," the man said in despair. "Red hair. About this tall. Moves very fast. Her name is Lucy." He rubbed his face.

He looked like he hadn't slept in a week, a little wild

around the eyes, and Olivia found that she was more concerned *for* him than frightened *of* him.

"I don't know how she gets out," he said, sounding half-hysterical. "I need to get a tracker for her, or something." Then he muttered something about how she'd probably get out of *that*, too.

"Has she been gone long?"

"Only a minute or two."

"She couldn't have gone far," Olivia said soothingly. "I'll check my backyard. Can she open the gates?"

"She doesn't have to," the man said cryptically. Then, in genuine alarm, "Is that your cat?"

Seltzer was coming from behind the house to greet his new royal subject, his big tail high in the air. Was her neighbor afraid of cats? Seltzer was a rather large cat, but very mellow. "This is Seltzer. He likes people and thinks he owns everything." It occurred to her that they hadn't exchanged their own names. "I'm Olivia."

"Ian," he said, and he reached his hand across the short fence to shake hers.

He had a good handshake; his long fingers were quite strong, but gentle. Olivia reminded herself that it was probably not a good idea to date neighbors, no matter how convenient and cute they were. Besides, with an almost-two-year-old daughter, there was probably a mom in the picture somewhere.

Seltzer gave Ian an expressive meow of greeting and rubbed possessively against the chain link fence between them.

Ian looked down at him with an expression of concern. "You…should probably keep him inside," he said hesitantly. "Wild animals, you know. Um. Owls."

"Owls?"

"There's a lot of local wildlife," Ian stammered.

Whether that was true or not, Olivia knew a lie when she heard one. "Well, let me go check my backyard," she said. "You said her name is Lucy?"

"Lucy," Ian agreed, then he called, "Lucy!" as he turned away again and wandered to the other side of his driveway.

Olivia left the box on her porch and opened the gate into her backyard, calling for Lucy and looking behind the raised beds. There was an interesting pile of garden tools that was half overgrown, but there were no hiding spaces big enough for a two-year-old. Seltzer followed her around for a while like a regal dog, then detoured to explore the back alley, squeezing himself through a gap in the wood slats.

Ian was doing a more thorough job in his own back-yard, looking under buckets and in other impossible places. He seemed to realize what he was doing as Olivia made a big circuit of her yard and returned to the fence boundary between them. "I'm going to go look inside again," he said nervously. "Maybe she's hiding and I missed her."

Olivia was starting to have reservations about this guy. He didn't seem dangerous, but maybe the child was a complete figment of his imagination. That was the kind of thing they ought to add to rental listings, she thought wryly. *All utilities included. Crazy guy next door. Imaginary daughter can walk through fences and hide under buckets.*

"Okay," she said reluctantly. "Good luck. I'm going to go unpack, but if you need anything, feel free to..."—did she want this guy to think he was welcome to come over? He was really good-looking, and even though her last few dates had been women, she liked guys just as well. She wasn't quite desperate enough for a date to encourage him by giving him her number—"...ah, holler?"

"Sure, sure," he replied, hurrying away.

Olivia told herself that she did not need more crazy in her life than she had already signed up for, teaching middle school, and returned to her own house.

Olivia had unpacked two boxes in the kitchen and the cabinets were still rattlingly empty when Seltzer gave his *Come Praise Me* cry from the back door.

She opened the door to see what hapless local wildlife he had caught and was startled to find that he was standing over a tiny, furry form. "Oh, not a squirrel, Seltzer. It's just a baby!"

She crouched to take away his prize and Seltzer marched past her with his tail high to approve the placement of his water and food in the new house.

The squirrel was alive and seemed unharmed, but was quivering in fear and curled in a tight, tiny ball with its fluffy red tail around it.

"Poor thing!" Olivia said, scooping the little creature into her hands before she could think to find a pair of gardening gloves in the box marked *outside stuff and electronics*. Hopefully, it wouldn't bite her; she knew that wild things were rarely grateful for human intervention. She could put it in one of the boxes she had just emptied, at least until it had gotten over the shock of being captured by the Great Hunter Seltzer.

Seltzer was very interested in this process.

"Leave it alone," Olivia scolded. "You've scared it enough."

There didn't seem to be any blood on it as she settled it into a few crumpled paper towels and its sides were moving with its quick, panicked breaths. Many of Seltzer's victims escaped unscathed; he was more interested in the thrill of the chase than the taste of his prey. It helped that Olivia bought him the most expensive cat food; he wasn't interested in anything less.

Olivia gently folded the top of the box down. It was marked *oven mitts, utensils, baking sheets*.

Hopefully, the baby squirrel just needed a few moments of rest and shelter before she could release it. *Hopefully*, it would be smart enough not to get caught again. Seltzer's collar had a bell, but it hadn't really dented his feline stalking skills.

Olivia turned to wash her hands before she folded up the rest of her empty boxes. She'd have to figure out when recycling and trash were picked up, and if her house came with any bins. There was no garage, but she hadn't gotten out past the back alley fence in her exploration yet.

Seltzer watched the box avidly and Olivia was relieved to hear scrabbling noises from within. She would be able to release it back out in the alley and there would be one less small helpless animal on her conscience.

But as she bent to open the box for a peek inside, poised to stop the escape of a tiny squirrel, the flaps sprang back and a small, red-headed girl pushed her way out and tipped herself over onto the floor.

"Uh-oh!" she said, upside-down.

CHAPTER 3

*I*an was sure that he was the worst father in the history of parenting.

Good fathers did not lose their almost-two-year-old squirrel-shifting toddlers on a near-daily basis.

He had exhausted all of Lucy's usual hiding places and tricks. She didn't seem to be in the yard, and Ian had been adamant about how she could never leave it. Maybe he'd put too much trust in her, thinking she understood things that she simply didn't have the capacity to comprehend. She was a smart kid; she had a big vocabulary for her age and she was already mostly potty trained, but maybe he put too much trust in her.

He hadn't even been trying to write this time, just answering nature's call because that was something his human body sometimes needed, and when he'd come out of the bathroom, her toys and her clothing had been abandoned.

And this time, not only had he failed to find Lucy with his mundane search, he'd looked like an absolute lunatic in front of the new neighbor. The distractingly hot new neighbor, with her silky black hair up in some kind of artfully fashionable messy bun. Even losing Lucy had not been able to completely keep him from noticing how beautiful her eyes were or how gracefully she moved…

…as she was helping him look for his missing daughter.

Because he was the most terrible dad ever.

"Lucy!" he cried in desperation. "I'll take you to the park! I'll give you ice cream! Honey, please come out!"

Silence.

Was she asleep somewhere? Was she simply out-stubborning him the way that only someone on the cusp of two could?

Ian reached for his last resort, deep in his own mind.

I need you.

He had to try again, more firmly.

I need you, **now**.

The response was slow, sluggish, and at first, intensely resistant.

Sleeping. It was a sense, more than an actual word.

It was like trying to wake Lucy on those rare occasions that she was sleeping hard and Ian needed to take her somewhere.

I need your help, he repeated insistently. *It can't wait.*

Slowly, his dragon woke.

Ian could feel it unfolding inside, sluggishly fighting back against its supernatural slumber.

It was easy to forget this half of himself. His dragon was sometimes asleep for days at a time.

Then it came completely awake and Ian felt like some part of his soul had been lit on fire, because with his dragon came his dragon's awareness of instinct.

Go, his dragon said firmly. *There! Now!*

Ian knew enough regular shifters—normal animals, not mythical—to know that for most of them, instinct was a confusing pull, a vague call, or an indistinct urge. But a dragon's magical power and age meant they were more anchored in instinct, and sensed its messages more strongly, if not more clearly.

There was next door, where the hot new neighbor was probably wishing she had blinds installed so that she could draw them as a barrier between them because he had not made anything like a good first impression. Was Lucy over there after all?

There! Now! Her! his dragon repeated. *I'm not going to argue with you about this.*

As much as he dreaded facing his neighbor again after the hash he'd made of their first meeting, especially with his dragon awake and dividing his attention, Ian needed Lucy back.

Ian retorted, *FINE,* and grabbed Lucy's dress. He was reassured that although instinct felt urgent, it didn't feel like *danger.*

The dress turned out to be unnecessary. When Olivia met him at the door, she was holding Lucy dressed in an adult baby-doll t-shirt, tied at the waist with what looked like a cat leash. The cap-sleeves hit her at the elbows.

Olivia, looking like she'd been hit in the face with a fish, gaped at Ian. "I'm guessing this is Lucy," she said, her eyes wide. "We were about to come find you." Lucy was in her arms, looking completely unharmed. She clapped her hands in glee.

"Lucy," Ian said, filled with relief. His daughter was safe, and his dragon, having dragged him to Olivia's door, had eased his iron grip on Ian's heart. Instinct was still saying *here* and *now,* but it was a pale shadow of the searing demand that it had been.

We are where we should be, now, his dragon said contentedly. There was an odd underlying sense of longing in its voice.

That gave him enough margin to wonder if Lucy had been a squirrel when Olivia found her…or was she only shocked because she'd been naked? Kids her age ran around naked all the time.

"Daddy!" Lucy said in joy, tilting forward out of Olivia's arms.

"Oh, thank heavens," Ian said, taking her and bouncing her up in the air. "You little monkey. You're not supposed to leave the yard, not ever!"

"I think you mean *squirrel*," Olivia said, "not monkey." That certainly answered the question of how Lucy had looked when she was found. Olivia's enchanting dark eyes were decidedly wild around the edges.

"I play wi kitty!" Lucy sang.

"I'm so sorry," Olivia said. "I think my cat caught your daughter." There was a quaver to her voice.

"She doesn't seem to be hurt," Ian assured her. "Anything ouchy, Lucy?" Great, he was an awful dad *and* he degenerated into babytalk.

You are not making a good impression, his dragon groused. *She will think we are not clever!*

Lucy shook her head vigorously. "Ah good," she said happily. "Ah good."

"You scared me," Ian said seriously.

Lucy leaned forward so that her forehead was touching his and patted him gently on the cheek. "Ah good."

It wasn't instinct that swelled in his heart over her tiny trusting hand on his face, only the same paternal warmth that any father would feel, and Ian could not quite keep from closing his eyes and holding her close for a moment of relief and love.

He opened his eyes to find Olivia staring at him with a

complicated expression of wonder, sympathy, and wild curiosity.

"Your daughter…"

"Lucy is a squirrel shifter."

Olivia closed her mouth like she was trying to hold in the questions that Ian knew she must have. Since his dragon was awake, he was able to tell if she was a shifter…and she definitely wasn't.

Judging by her stunned face, she hadn't known about them at all.

"Squill," Lucy agreed.

"Okay," Olivia said slowly, like she was trying to convince herself that it was. "Okay, she's a squirrel *shifter.* That's probably pretty complicated."

Ian gave a cough of laughter and Lucy nodded. "Ah good," she said gravely. "Ah good." She spotted Seltzer and made grabby hands in the cat's direction. "Kitty!"

Ian should take Lucy and go, he thought, but for some reason, even thinking about that made instinct swell again and insist, *here, now.*

Lucy is safe, he told his dragon. *Why do we still need to be here?*

She's the one, his dragon said, sounding deeply content. *She is our heart and our hoard. Now we will be complete.*

That was the last thing Ian needed right now.

CHAPTER 4

"*D*o you want a drink?" Olivia offered impulsively. Her hot new next-door neighbor had just sprung the existence of were-squirrels on her, and although it did explain that hot neighbor's bizarre behavior, she had *questions*.

"I'd love that," Ian said. Lucy was still leaning for Seltzer, reaching her hands towards the puzzled, fluffy cat. Did the feline understand that the little girl was the same as the squirrel that had been in the *interesting box*? He looked confused, and Olivia didn't blame him.

Olivia wished that she had something in her fridge other than a few warm sodas. She didn't drink much, and it was the middle of the afternoon, but she definitely felt like something stronger was called for.

"Lucy and I will share," Ian said. There were no tables or chairs, but he settled into a cross-legged seat on the floor gracefully. "No, Lucy, I don't think the kitty wants to play."

Seltzer, apparently determined to make a liar out of him, immediately marched over to Ian and rubbed against his knee before attempting to climb up and see Lucy.

"Seltzer," Olivia said warningly, but he was a cat, so it did no good.

Ian and Olivia watched carefully as the cat and child greeted each other, both cautious and curious. Lucy patted his head, a little hard, but Seltzer leaned into it and began to purr.

Ian seemed to sag with relief, and he let Lucy out of his arms to sit by herself with Seltzer. Olivia thought to get one of Seltzer's cat fascinators, a fishing pole with a weighted feather, and they immediately began to play.

"He's a nice cat," Ian observed as Olivia brought him an orange soda that was her only soda choice.

"He's a sweetheart," Olivia agreed, popping her own soda open. "When he isn't trying to eat the neighborhood children, apparently. So…are you a squirrel shifter, too? Or is it a werewolf thing? Is this a hazard of being bitten by local wildlife that I didn't realize?"

"It's genetic," Ian said, sipping the overflow from the lip of his can when it opened. "Her mother is a squirrel shifter."

"Like a shape shifter? That's…just a thing? Are there many of you?"

"There are a lot of shifters," Ian said gruffly. "And a lot of different kinds. You can understand why we stay a secret, though."

"Sure," Olivia agreed. "Evil scientist labs. A lot of awkward questions. Never knowing what species to check on medical forms." Now that the shock of it had mostly passed, she was starting to like the idea. She'd always loved fairy tales with shape changers. "Are you going to get in trouble for telling me? Is it like…a secret society?"

Ian was watching Lucy and Seltzer rather than Olivia, and he looked a bit like he was fighting to concentrate. "Kind of?" He looked back at her. "I mean, it *is* a secret.

And shifters have an extra sense, an instinct, and we can recognize each other, but we don't know what kind of shifter the other person is. It's considered impolite to ask."

"Well, recognizing each other sounds handy," Olivia said. "And you can…control your shapeshifting? It's not a full moon thing? Do you get an insatiable hunger for acorns?" She laughed and recognized that it sounded a little shocky. "I'm sorry, I'm dragging a whole lot of media conditioning in here. It's probably all terribly inaccurate."

To her relief, Ian chuckled. "Most of it is pretty wrong, yeah. No full moons, no insatiable…hungers." The way he trailed off the last word gave Olivia all kinds of inappropriate ideas. He shook his head as if to clear it. "Instinct… instinct is its own special thing. It's a little unpredictable, but along with telling us about other shifters, it can tell us about danger, or…about *good* things."

Olivia tried to decide what his tone really meant. It was pointed, she thought, and he was focused on her again. She took a sip of her soda because she wasn't sure what to say, and nearly choked when she got more bubbles than she expected. She coughed and had to clear her throat.

Ian went on. "Instinct is like an *urge*, but it doesn't come with any explanation. It's a pull, with a really strong feeling of *should* or *should not*, but it doesn't tell you *why*, or *how*."

Seltzer had tired of the game and was ignoring the feather, despite Lucy's efforts to entice him with it and Lucy was resorting to poking him with it directly. "Don't hurt the kitty," Ian warned. "He might not want to play anymore."

Indeed, Seltzer hissed a mild warning when Lucy got too forward with the feather, then got to his feet and wandered elegantly away. Lucy started to follow, but Ian called her back. "Want a sip of soda, Lucy? It's orange!"

Lucy was distracted, first with a careful sip of the soda,

and then with the box that Olivia had first put her in as a squirrel. "Imma car!" she said, crawling back into it. "Vroom, vroom!"

When Olivia was sure that she wasn't going to tip over in it, she returned her attention to Ian, and caught him staring at her.

"So…instinct," she said, trying to remember where the conversation had left off. "Tells you good things."

Ian nodded. "You're a good thing," he said quietly. "You feel...trustworthy."

So he *was* a shifter. But he'd been clear that Lucy's mother was what made her a squirrel, so apparently, he was something else entirely? "Well, I like that," she said lightly. "Being trustworthy is an admirable quality."

Lucy was babbling happily in the car-box, moving the flaps up and down like they were wings and describing her destinations to Ian and Olivia as she went. Olivia understood a few of the words, but most of it was a conversational stream of cute, random sounds. The little girl didn't seem to expect a lot of interaction from her audience.

"So, ah, welcome to Nickel City. What brought you here?" Ian asked.

"I have a teaching contract with the Nickel City middle school. I teach science." Olivia wondered where magic fit in that curriculum. Did it follow rules? Clearly not conservation of mass! Squirrel-Lucy hadn't weighed anything close to human-Lucy's mass.

"That sounds like fun," Ian said.

Olivia didn't think he was kidding, but she wasn't sure. "I try to make sure we do a lot of experiments," she said. "Like a Latina Bill Nye the Science Guy."

Ian gave a guffaw of laughter.

"What do you do?" Olivia asked. She really wanted to ask more about Lucy's squirrel-shifting mother. Was she still in the picture? Ian didn't have a ring, but people were in all kinds of relationships these days that weren't as official as marriage.

Was she already thinking about this guy as a dating possibility? Shape-shifting squirrel daughter and all? She didn't usually date people with kids at all, and this seemed *extra* complicated with sprinkles on top.

"I'm a writer," Ian said sheepishly.

"That's so cool," Olivia said. "Have you written something I would know? James Bond, perhaps?"

"Wrong Ian," he laughed. "Wrong genre."

"I thought you were a little young," Olivia teased. "What do you write?"

"Science fiction," Ian admitted, like he expected Olivia to think less of him for it.

"You have a book out?" Olivia only thought afterward that it might not be the safest of topics. Maybe saying he was a writer was a bit of a bluff and she was calling it. Being an author certainly explained that slightly wild mad-scientist look that he had.

Of course, having a squirrel-shifting toddler would explain that look, too.

Ian looked like an adorable mix of embarrassment and pride. "The first book is out and did pretty well. It's a trilogy and I'm working on book two now." He grimaced. "I've already gotten two extensions to my deadline and I'm worried I'm going to have to return my advance if I can't get Lucy to let me write."

"That sounds tough," Olivia said sympathetically. "Especially since…"

On cue, Lucy turned into a red squirrel, squirmed from Olivia's oversized shirt, fell out of the car-box, and shot straight up the wall.

Seltzer had been able to disdain the feather, but he was

not equal to containing his chase instinct with a tiny, chattering squirrel. Olivia wasn't even sure if he tried.

Olivia and Ian both leapt to their feet, and Ian's orange soda splashed onto the carpet as he lunged for his daughter. Olivia's can dropped straight down as she dashed to catch Seltzer, who was scrambling after Lucy but unable to follow. He danced along the baseboard on his hind feet, his feather-like tail lashing behind him.

Olivia wasn't sure how, but Lucy was on the top of the curtain rod, chittering in what appeared to be glee.

"Lucy!" Ian cried. "Get down here! Fingers and feet!"

Olivia caught Seltzer and tried not to laugh. She locked the cat in the bedroom and returned to find Lucy landing on her father's shoulder, where she transformed smoothly into a little girl, laughing and hugging his head like it had all been a delightful game. Seltzer protested from behind the shut door.

"Let's get you dressed," Ian said with a suffering sigh. He'd brought a dress with him that fit Lucy considerably better than Olivia's T-shirt and Lucy was soon demurely back to two (bare) feet while Olivia hastily mopped up the spilled orange soda with paper towels.

"I'm so sorry about the carpet," Ian said, stooping to help her.

"It will come out!" Olivia said. "There wasn't much left in either can."

Lucy seemed considerably more tired now, and when Ian caught Olivia looking at her curiously, he explained, "Shifting takes a lot of energy and she's usually taking a nap about now. It's like this a lot. One hundred percent on and then one hundred percent off. We should probably head home."

Seltzer was still yowling from the bedroom.

Ian gathered Lucy back up into his arms and she

burrowed her head into his neck and sighed. Olivia was not sure she had ever seen anything more adorable. Well, maybe Lucy as a squirrel, all fuzzy and bright-eyed. "Maybe you'll get a chance to do some writing," she said. "I can image that's really challenging."

Ian bounced Lucy into a more comfortable position, nodding. "There's hope on the horizon, too," he said optimistically. "I just found out that there's a place opening up for us in the local shifter day care. Lucy starts tomorrow."

"There's a shifter day care?" Olivia wasn't sure why that surprised her so much. Clearly, shifter children would be a handful. "That sounds amazing."

"It's short-handed," Ian said. "I was on the waitlist for nearly a month and the spot we got is just part-time. Cherry's been trying to hire someone…" he looked up at her with sudden intensity. "You wouldn't happen to be looking for work?"

Olivia gave a half-laugh. "I was thinking about picking up something temporary until school starts next month. Waitressing, or something."

"You were great with Lucy," Ian said, but he said it as if he was arguing with someone else in his head.

"I put her in a box and she turned into a little girl," Olivia pointed out. "I'm not sure there was much to it beyond that."

"Owevy," Lucy said sleepily. Olivia thought it might be her name, but she only understood about one word in ten from the little girl.

Ian sighed like he'd lost his internal debate. "Can I give you Cherry's number? I mean, it's kind of forward of me, and I wouldn't normally do this, but…"

"That desperate for childcare?" Olivia chuckled. "I didn't have anything else lined up yet, and it might be fun. Does it pay well?"

Ian chuckled. "Probably not. And it will be terrifically hard and the hours might be awful and I'm really not doing a good job of selling it, am I?"

Olivia put the number in her phone anyway. Nickel City was turning out to be full of surprises.

CHAPTER 5

*I*an woke in a cold sweat from a nightmare of fire.

The first thing he did was hold his breath and listen. Had Lucy woken him? Was she in danger? He grasped for his dragon, for instinct to give him a clue, and found sleepy, unconcerned comfort. It was just conscious enough to reassure him that nothing was wrong.

Slowly, his heart stopped pounding, and Ian sat up to check and make sure he hadn't singed the sheets in his sleep as the dream slowly faded from his brain; he sometimes lost control of his dragon's power of fire when he let his emotions slip and his dragon slept.

He rolled to his feet and padded out to the next room to check on Lucy, still sleeping peacefully in her toddler bed, arms akimbo. A crib had been useless since she started shifting, months ago, and the nightly battle of getting her tired enough to stay in the bed was certainly a thing now. Ian stood for a moment looking down at her. How could something so little and helpless be such a powerful force in his life? She had him wrapped around her tiny fingers completely, and he'd never been so happy.

Or so exhausted.

He wanted to wake her, to chase the last of his nightmare from his mind with her joyous giggles and affectionate hugs...but it was still early, and this was her first day of day care. She needed all the rest she could get.

Or more to the point, the day care didn't need a tired, wound-up version of her for her first day.

And Ian needed a shower.

He listened carefully after he started the water, worried that the noise of the pipes would wake Lucy, but she slept on, and Ian's dragon joined her in slumber.

Ian shucked off his sweat-damp shirt and shorts and stepped into a shower that wasn't nearly as hot as he wanted it to be; he'd turned down the water heater to protect Lucy and of all the things he missed being a dad— a full night's sleep, writing time, uninterrupted meals, five minutes of privacy—he missed scalding hot showers the most.

His dream had been hot, wild, and worrisome, and it stirred up vague and unhappy memories of his childhood. Ian leaned his head against the cool tile of the shower and let himself remember.

As far as Ian knew, when most shifters, Lucy included, first started shifting, their animals were young like they were. Lucy's squirrel was a baby squirrel. His friend Roderick's wolf was a puppy at first, like his daughter Gabby's was now. Children grew up in tandem with their animals.

But dragons were *generational* shifters, slipping fully developed from one human host to another when their mortal bodies failed. Ian had later learned from his dragon they usually took adult hosts, willing and capable of accepting a magical passenger in exchange for power and the ability to shift.

Ian had made no such choice. He hadn't been capable of it.

He had abruptly become a dragon when he was four, somewhat late for a shifter to emerge, and he didn't have an infant creature who grew and developed along with his human half, he suddenly had a fully-grown dragon in his head who was frustrated by his lack of development and manual dexterity, with several lifetime's worth of experience that it didn't hesitate to use. Ian wanted to play with trucks and build forts. His dragon wanted to discuss finance and stimulating literature. Ian was still eating dirt, his dragon was constantly outraged by his lack of common sense. It had been a terribly unbalanced relationship...and sometimes, still, he lost control.

Ian had terrifying half-memories of losing a grip on his power, of standing in waist-high flames listening to screams, of losing himself to his dragon, who seemed to alternate in his recall between a blanket of comfort and reassurance, and a bitter critic.

His dream blurred with the memories. He'd set their apartment on fire and Ian knew that he was the reason that his family had moved away to live in the wilderness, and that later his parents split because of his abnormal and impossible shifter powers.

Eventually, he grew up enough to manage a tentative partnership with his inner animal. His parents weren't shifters, though they had always known about the magical world that was underlying to the mundane. His father, who had always been distant, died when he was still in middle school, a year or two after he left, and his mother, who had never been particularly warm, became distant and cold. Ian told himself that it was to protect her own heart.

They moved back to Nickel City when Ian went into high school, confident at last that he could socialize and keep his secrets safe in the little town with a proportionately high population of shifters. His mother made it clear that moving back to such a small and uncultured town was a great step down socially, that all of her life had been a series of devoted sacrifices for Ian, and that his being a dragon was a terrible burden to her. He was glad she chose to move away from Nickel City as soon as Ian was old enough to live alone, and the first thing Ian had done as a father was vow that he would never let Lucy live with that same kind of awful pressure, no matter what she turned out to be.

I didn't remember how to be a child, his dragon agreed, surprising him with consciousness. When instinct was quiet, as it was now, his dragon could come and go silently. Then, to Ian's further shock, it added thoughtfully, *I wasn't always understanding.*

His dragon often spent his time in a deep slumber, or quietly in the back of Ian's head, which was how Ian could best balance getting on with his life, because otherwise, there was a constant underlying sense of supernatural feedback, like a microphone too close to a speaker. They were often at odds and Ian knew too well how inconclusive and ineffective he looked when he was busy arguing with the voice in his head. It was like having a much older sibling in his brain with him, constantly trying to tell him what to do with all the superiority of greater wisdom and age.

There were few things that they agreed upon at once— loving Lucy was one of those.

And now, for the first time in a long time, they had a new purpose that they agreed on: to win Olivia.

Even without instinct trying to drag him along, Ian could not stop thinking about his new next-door neighbor.

Olivia.

The first thing he noticed about her was how lively she was, with expressive dark eyes and a beautiful mouth in constant motion. If she wasn't speaking, she was smiling, or frowning thoughtfully, or licking her lips.

Even if it wasn't boiling hot, the shower was definitely not cold enough to stop his body's reaction to that memory. What would she taste like? Ian wondered. What would she feel like in his arms?

We should find out, his dragon suggested eagerly.

The shower was abruptly considerably more full of steam and Ian turned off the faucet and wrenched his thoughts back to discipline. Instinct or not, he needed to keep himself under control.

Otherwise, he would do nothing but endanger her.

CHAPTER 6

Olivia's air mattress had a tiny leak and she had to get up several times during an uncomfortable night to blow it back up, chasing her sleeping bag over the slippery surface. She was going to need a real bed in very short order. Particularly because she had to keep shooing Seltzer off of it. His claws were not going to help her ability to keep it inflated long enough to sleep.

As if that was not enough to keep her awake, every few moments, her brain would remind her that there was a squirrel-shifting toddler living next door, with a really hot dad who was also a shifter, even though it was clear that he wasn't a squirrel himself.

A *mystery* shifter.

And it all meant that there was magic in the world. Real magic, and people who could shift into animals, and if that was possible, what else was? Happy ever afters? Wishes coming true?

Olivia finally got up at the crack of dawn. Whether it was the sagging mattress or carrying all of her heavy boxes in without pause after three days of marathon driving, her back was sore and she rifled through her boxes to find some ibuprofen and her running shoes. It would be good to get out and get the lay of the land.

The neighborhood was even nicer in the early morning than it had been in the sweltering afternoon, with a cool breeze that made Olivia's jog a delight. She found the middle school where she would be working and neighborhood after neighborhood of cute little houses. There were a lot of trees to provide comfortable shade, and a few quaint corner stores. A ham and cheese croissant from a tiny coffee cart was mediocre, but she shouldn't expect gourmet quality for coffee cart prices anywhere. She'd have to take the car to get downtown, and to the real tourist sites, but the more she saw of it, the more Olivia liked Nickel City.

When she made it back to Crescent Avenue, with the help of the GPS on her phone after she'd gotten hopelessly turned around on the random, twisting roads, Ian was in the alley leaning over to buckle Lucy into her car seat. She resisted the urge to fix her hair as she jogged past. She was un-showered and sweaty and if this was the worst that he saw of her as a next-door neighbor, she'd count herself lucky. And even though Olivia thought that Ian seemed interested in her, the word he'd used with her was *trustworthy*.

Trustworthy was something you called an aunt, not a hot date.

"Owivah!" Lucy cried, catching sight of her through the straps that Ian was trying to get around her.

Ian banged his head on the car standing up too fast. "Olivia!" he said with a big grin. "Hi."

"Hi," Olivia said, slowing to a stop. She was more breathless now than she'd been while jogging. "Hi, Lucy!"

"I'm gwanna abe air."

Olivia looked at Ian for translation.

"Day care. We're going to day care. I'm pretty sure she doesn't know what that is yet, but doesn't it sound fun, Lucy?"

Ian had a slightly desperate look around his eyes, like he wasn't at all sure of what he was trying to convince Lucy.

"That sounds wonderful," Olivia said encouragingly. If Lucy was at day care, her golden-eyed dad would be home alone allllllll day.

She reminded herself firmly that Ian was doing day care to get writing done, and they had barely gotten past first name introductions, and besides, she was supposed to be looking for a job of her own in order to pay off the exorbitant lease she was stuck in.

But when she caught Ian's gaze before he turned back to finish buckling Lucy in, she thought he might be having the same kinds of thoughts that she was; his ears were pink and Olivia imagined that she saw a whiff of smoke coming off of them.

"Owely come to abe air?" Lucy suggested. "Sezzer?"

"I'm pretty sure Olivia doesn't want to go to day care with you," Ian said with a laughing sideways glance. "And Seltzer has to stay here."

"Sezzer abba liver kitty wizzle."

"That's right," Ian said kindly, though Olivia only understood two of her words: kitty, and Sezzer as the name she called Seltzer. "Abba liver wizzle," Lucy repeated gravely.

Ian shut the door on her and for a moment, they were almost alone, a car door separating them from Lucy.

Olivia realized that she was loitering shamelessly. She could easily have jogged right on by with a wave, and instead, she was blushing and flirting—badly, she feared—with Ian, who looked like he was searching for words like she was. "So, ah, good luck," she said. "With day care." She remembered that he'd given her the number and suggested it as a place to get some quick temporary work. "Tiny Paws, right? The owner is Cherry?"

"Daddy! Daddy!" Lucy's call through the window was muffled.

"Yeah," Ian said. "Tiny Paws. Cherry. I'll talk to her about the job. If you want."

"That would be great, thanks," Olivia said, only wondering after she'd said so if it would be. Did she want to work at a day care? Would it be too weird to date Ian if she was watching his daughter? Was she really thinking about dating this guy so soon?

"Daddy! Daddy!" Lucy cried more desperately. "I have to go potty!"

"Whoops," Ian said, turning back to open the car door with trained urgency. "I guess we're not going to Tiny Paws quite yet this morning…"

Olivia backed away to let him get Lucy deftly out of the car seat and waved. "Well, catch you later," she said, waving.

"Bye!" Lucy cried, as he carried her into the house, praising her for letting him know. "Bye, Owevellea!"

Olivia floated back to her own house, smiling foolishly. She swept Seltzer up into her arms, to his protest, and danced around the empty living room until he purred in protest and struggled to get loose because it was too undignified to admit that he liked it.

The cat's claws scratched at her and Olivia let him go, feeling like her bubble had been abruptly popped. She'd had crazy crushes before, she reminded herself, and just look where that had gotten her. It was easier to think, when

Ian wasn't standing there all handsome and wholesome and ready to climb, and easier to remember that she wasn't a good judge of character.

He'd called her *trustworthy*. But was *he* trustworthy? And was she really thinking about giving him her heart already?

CHAPTER 7

Ian peeled a protesting Lucy from his body. "Lucy, honey, you have to stay here right now. Gabby's going to be here. You like Gabby! Did you see the bear? Look at the bear!"

Ian thought that the bear, with his "'BEAR' FEET PLEASE!" sign and weirdly human toes was honestly a little horrifying, but he was desperate to distract Lucy, who had realized that day care meant that Ian was planning to leave her alone, possibly *forever*, and was doing her level best to grow extra limbs to cling to him with.

Cherry, the owner of Tiny Paws, seemed to materialize at the inner entrance to the day care, standing just behind a child safety gate. "Hi, Lucy!" she called kindly. "Do you know how to use a telephone? I have a phone call, and I think it's for you!"

She was holding a plastic phone to her ear. "Yes," she said. "Lucy's right here, I'll see if she wants to talk to you."

Lucy stared at her. "Who it is?" she asked cautiously.

Cherry cast a look at Ian for help, and he wracked his brain as he closed the distance to the short fence. "Maybe it's Grandma?" he suggested. "Do you want to talk to Grandma?"

Lucy buried her face in his neck and clung tighter.

"No, no," Cherry said quickly. "It's not Grandma, it's Green Dog and he's telling me jokes! Have you met Green Dog, Lucy?"

Lucy shook her head against Ian's chin.

"Green Dog is inside the day care," Cherry said coaxingly. "But you can talk to him on the phone first."

Lucy peeled one hand off of Ian to take the phone that she offered.

"'Come on in, Lucy,'" Cherry said, in a growly dog voice. "'We've got lots of fun games.'"

Lucy giggled and smiled, holding the phone flat to the side of her face.

"'Do you like dogs?'" Cherry asked.

"I like kitties," Lucy said into the phone. "Sezzer."

"Seltzer is the cat that just moved in next door," Ian explained. That reminded him: "Are you still looking for some more hands? My next-door neighbor has a few weeks before she starts teaching and she was looking for some temporary work." It felt as awkward to suggest it as it had been to tell Olivia about the job, but his dragon was adamant.

Get on with it, his dragon prodded. *This is what happens next.*

Instinct was like standing in a fast-moving stream, dragging at all of his limbs and thoughts. Ian wanted to dig his heels in out of sheer stubbornness and having his dragon nagging in his ear didn't really help.

"What does she teach? Is she a shifter?" Cherry wanted to know. Lucy was babbling into the phone now, more interested in keeping a cadence of conversation than in saying actual words.

Ian shook his head. "Middle school science, and, no. She's actually completely new to the concept of shifters, but she's adaptable and great with Lucy and…" Ian wasn't sure how to explain his certainty that Olivia would be a perfect fit.

"Instinct tells you she'd work out for me?" Cherry guessed. *Cherry* was definitely not new to the concept of shifters.

"Yeah," Ian said, and he realized that he was smiling really stupidly, because that had reminded him of everything else that instinct was suggesting. Olivia might be his *one, his happiness forever.* The idea was still strange and terrifying.

"I won't lie," Cherry said wryly, "I could use another warm body in here. I've had to turn away a couple of babies because I don't have the staff ratio the state requires, and shifter kids really require more attention than most. If you think she could hack it, I'm willing to give her a shot."

"I'll let her know," Ian said, filled with relief. "I know she's up for it."

See, his dragon pointed out. *I told you it would work out. You're so resistant for no reason.*

Lucy was relaxed enough now, playing with the phone, that Ian attempted to hand her over to Cherry—with disastrous results.

She fell out of her dress with a squirrel squeak and clambered up Ian's arm to hide behind him.

Cherry, kindly, did not laugh at him as he did a TikTok-worthy dance trying to get Lucy out from the collar of his shirt as she tried to burrow down the back of his neck.

Finally, he got Lucy gently into both hands and he crouched down on the floor with her. "Fingers and feet," he told her firmly. "Let me give you a big hug as a little girl."

She sulkily shifted back and Ian deftly got her dress back over her head before she had time to fling her arms around as much of him as she could reach.

"You know I'll come back," he reminded her. "You know I love you. You know you'll be safe and have fun here. I promise."

She was tearful but tired now, and she nodded her head against him. "Pwomise," she echoed.

"I'll miss you," Ian told her, feeling an ache in his chest. It was only for a day, he reminded himself. Lucy would forgive him.

He hugged her until she reluctantly let go, and when he finally stood up, his legs had aches from crouching uncomfortably for so long.

Lucy let Cherry lift her up over the gate, and Ian told himself that she wouldn't cry for long after he left.

Beyond the gate, he heard an owl shriek, a puppy yip, and someone shout, "Don't eat that!" as a baby started crying.

What on earth was he suggesting that Olivia get into?

CHAPTER 8

$\mathscr{O}$livia hadn't been this nervous before an interview since she first started teaching. She told herself that it didn't really matter, it was a temporary job, she already had a contract with the school district to step into, and there were plenty of help wanted signs in downtown Nickel City if this one fell through.

But for some reason, she really wanted to impress Cherry…and maybe Ian, too, if she was being honest.

Olivia wasn't sure what it was about Ian that intrigued her so much. He was good-looking, but Olivia had known better-built beach jocks and more attractive girls with brighter eyes. He seemed smart enough, and funny and wry, and he was certainly kind and had just the right amount of confidence, but Olivia wasn't sure why she was so smitten, despite all of her better sense. Maybe it was just the way that he looked at her, like he had never seen anything like her, like she was the most interesting and appealing creature he'd ever met.

And the way that he looked at his daughter melted all her defenses.

So, when he said that he'd talked to Cherry and that she was interested in seeing her resume, Olivia felt obliged to make a good impression, to live up to whatever it was that he had told the owner of the day care. She found the box with her computer and after a day figuring out how to set up her printer so she could make a hardcopy of her resume, called the number Ian gave her. Cherry invited her to drop by the following day.

Cherry herself met Olivia at the door. Olivia had expected an old woman, because Ian said she'd been watching shifter kids for years before opening an official day care, and Cherry certainly had streaks of white in her dark hair. But she also had streaks of electric purple tipped in pink, and she was wearing a T-shirt with Animal from The Muppets playing drums. She had very fit arms and a sunny smile. Dark eyes smiled from a well-lined face.

The day care itself looked like a saloon from the outside, and Olivia hadn't been sure that she was in the right place until she got close enough to see the bright tissue paper that had been taped up behind the windows as a privacy screen.

There was an electric lock with a camera and speaker at the front door, and when she was admitted, it opened onto a narrow little lobby lined with a bench on one side under the windows and cubbies and hooks on the other. About half of them had bags or backpacks hanging up, in cute animal shapes or covered with popular cartoons. There was a chaos of shoes and sandals underneath the bench and a big cartoon bear commanded them not to wear shoes inside. There was a sock lost-and-found pinned to the board.

At one end of the entry corridor, there was a baby gate across an entrance back into the main day care, and Olivia could hear expected sounds of children playing and calling to each other, the banging of toys, and the brief squalling of a baby.

Cherry took Olivia's resume and sat down on the bench to flip through, clearly skimming it.

Olivia recognized that it was largely not applicable—a master's of science degree, several teaching certificates, some summer camp counselor experience, but also a lot of waitress jobs and three years at a home improvement warehouse while she was paying her way through school. She hadn't bothered putting her photography experience down.

"I don't have a lot of specialized *early* education training," she confessed, not sure if she should sit beside Cherry or continue to politely stand. "But I have taken child CPR, and I can change a diaper."

Cherry laughed good-naturedly. "Diaper-changing is a big part of our criteria," she confided, folding the front page of the resume back over and putting it beside her on the bench. "That, and general patience. The kids—especially *these* kids—can take a lot of energy, really what I'm looking for is someone who can step into the ring and stay cool and keep going for a whole day."

Olivia hoped her nod looked self-assured and cheerful.

Cherry looked hard at Olivia. "You know that these are particularly special children," she said carefully.

Olivia nodded. "Shifters," she said in wonder. She'd gone from not even knowing about them to applying for a job raising them in just a few days…and it felt like the most natural progression in the world. Why wouldn't there be magic and wonder in the world, just beyond a flimsy shroud of normalcy?

"Not all of them are shifting yet," Cherry said, "but many of them are. They are faster and stronger than most children their age, and they can't control themselves, or their animals, very well at all. We have to teach them all of the things that regular toddlers are learning, and how to manage their other form, all at once. It is imperative to protect their secrets, and keep them safe."

Olivia nodded again. She felt like she was being considered for membership in a secret society, or an elite government agency.

"This job is messy, and these kids have huge feelings. It can be heartbreaking, and frustrating, and exhausting," Cherry warned. "I pay minimum wage plus three an hour, there are no benefit packages for temporary work, and I can't afford to replace clothing that gets accidentally damaged by the kids with claws."

"I can do it," Olivia said, more confidently than she felt. It would be for less than a month. She could handle anything for that long. "That's fine."

"I don't have instinct to tell me if you would work out," Cherry said frankly. "I have to go with my human gut and common sense, but both of those tell me that you'd be a good fit here, and that our kids would be safe in your hands." She bounced to her feet and extended a hand. "If you have any questions, please don't hesitate to ask any of us. You'll always be part of a team, here."

Part of a team. Olivia stuffed back the swell of emotions that came with that statement, not sure she could deal with them now as she followed Cherry back into a scene of chaos.

CHAPTER 9

It was like stepping into a cartoon.

The building had clearly once been a saloon, leaning hard into a turn-of-the-century mining Wild West aesthetic, but it had since been refinished with colorful shelves and low dividers with padded corners. Mirrors above the shelves made the room look even bigger than it was. There were books—mostly board books—and stuffed animals and games and building blocks and plastic food strewn everywhere. Backing the coat room was a row of cages, holding birds, lizards, and small rodents.

Olivia thought that was a sensible addition to a day care where some of the children could be animals, to help protect their secrets and provide plausible deniability.

There was a narrow hallway in the back that opened into a sunny courtyard that Olivia just got a glimpse of before she was meeting a young woman with strawberry-blonde hair and a colorful tiered skirt.

"This is Addison," Cherry said.

"The kids call me Addy," she said. "I answer to either! Is Cherry throwing you feet first in the soup?"

"Soup! I'm baking soup!" a child wearing an apron cried, waving a wooden spoon.

Addison had a baby owl in the crook of one elbow, and a squirrel on her shoulder who took one look at Olivia and gave a trill of recognition.

Before Olivia could brace herself, the squirrel was springing right for her face. Olivia dropped her purse and scrambled to catch her, sure that reflexively hitting the creature out of the air would be worse than dropping her. Lucy—because that was who it had to be!—barely weighed anything. It was like catching a half-shaved tribble with tiny, scratching claws.

Before Olivia could even celebrate not fumbling her, Lucy was climbing wildly up to her shoulder and making happy laps around her neck, chittering and dragging her tail under Olivia's chin.

"She's certainly happy to see you!" Addison said with a laugh. "Welcome to the chaos!"

There was a squall of outrage from the back courtyard, followed by yelling, and Cherry hurried to find out what fresh disaster had happened there.

"We're about to start lunch," Addison said. She stooped to put the owl on the ground, where it turned into a baby girl who bobbled three steps and fell on her face. "It will be nice to have an extra set of hands today!" She had the same bubbly kind of warmth that Cherry did, and Olivia hoped that she wouldn't come across as too grim to work in such a joyous place. It was certainly a welcome change from the sullen pre-teens of middle school.

The little owl girl, Amy, was righted and dressed, and Lucy was coaxed down from Olivia's shoulder to join her. "Owia!" she said happily, then she looked around, puzzled. "Oweveh! Sezzer? Kitty?"

"I didn't bring Seltzer with me," Olivia said apologetically. She could just imagine what Seltzer would make of this place.

A slight child with brown curls a little older than Lucy was carrying a bendy sapling in a pot that looked entirely too heavy for her to lift. Was it a fake tree? She shyly held it out to Olivia, but when Olivia tried to take it, the girl snatched it away and retreated behind a bookshelf to stare accusingly at Olivia while she tried to figure out what she'd done wrong.

"She just wants to show you," Addison explained, dragging a high chair away from the wall. "That's Oette."

Cherry came in with three older children who ran to help get lunches together for all of the children.

"I wan googur!" one of them exclaimed.

"Yogurt," Addison translated for her.

There were only a dozen kids, though Olivia saw another woman holding a fussy baby just past a curtain in one of the corners of the open building.

She would not have guessed that many children could be as much work as they were. The youngest ones required help eating, but the older ones were almost as demanding, needing assistance opening their yogurt, cleaning up spills, being reminded to keep their hands to themselves, to sit in their chairs, to stop crawling around on the floor.

It was loud in the high-ceilinged room, as they called to each other and shrieked in laughter whenever an accident happened. Amy pounded on her tray and screamed after spilling all of her food onto the floor. Gabby, a brown-skinned toddler in the next high chair, tried to hand over her own crackers and dried peas.

Olivia found herself in near-constant motion, wiping faces and hands, opening snack containers, closing snack containers, picking up dropped napkins, helping kids with forks and baggies and water bottles. Every time she turned around, someone had their hand in the air, "Miss Teacher? Miss Owivey?" They all said her name differently.

The table with the oldest kids had a pitcher of water and they took turns overfilling their dixie cups and playing in the puddles. Cherry had disappeared into the back to take a phone call, and Addy took laughing charge of the room.

One of the kids abruptly turned into a puppy and lapped spilled water up off the floor.

"Fingers and feet for snack time," Addison reminded her firmly.

The little girl flowed back up into human form, all of her clothing neatly in place, and sheepishly took her seat.

"I have top porn!" a little boy named Gil told her proudly.

Olivia was confused and alarmed until she realized that he was trying to say popcorn. "That looks…delicious." She hadn't thought to pack a lunch, and when her stomach growled, Jennifer, the puppy shifter, giggled and knocked over her water glass.

Addison slipped her a granola bar and Olivia gratefully devoured it as she went to open a container for Tara, a quiet, dark-haired girl with her hand patiently in the air.

Oette ate nothing and no one handed her any lunch. Olivia tried to offer her crackers, but she shook her head. She simply sat at the table with the others, swinging her legs and scooting the plant around in circles in front of her.

Olivia didn't have a single moment to feel self-conscious, or worry about whether she was doing anything wrong. She flitted from table to high chair and back, and the moment that lunch was done, they were setting up for a messy craft, and from there it was quiet time.

Olivia thought that might mean a little respite, but

getting them down for quiet time was itself a herculean task.

As soon as everyone was down on their mats, Jennifer needed to go potty. (Olivia went with her, but apparently only as a supervisor; her presence was insisted upon, but not actually required.) Gabby needed a diaper change. She came back from that to find an armadillo who turned out to be Gil, rolling around between the mats. He needed to be chased down, dressed again, and put firmly back in his space.

Amy wanted to bounce as an owl on her mat until she fell over in place and was a completely unconscious, naked little girl.

Oette seemed perfectly happy to lie on her mat staring up at the ceiling without blinking the entire time, her potted plant in arm's reach.

Addison showed Olivia where the blankets were and pointed out the cleaning supplies, quietly going over the procedure for letting people in. She had to download an app to her phone that accessed the security camera out front.

"Only vetted parents, of course," Addison emphasized. "You'll get to know them all in a few days, but if you ever have any questions, get me, or Cherry, or Shea."

Some of the older kids whispered with each other the entire quiet time, but a few fell asleep, and just as Olivia thought that she might be able to sit down for a moment or get a drink or check her phone, Addison started letting the oldest ones up to play in the courtyard.

Shea, when they finally met, was a shy Asian woman that gave Olivia a completely different feeling than Addison or Cherry. Where they were full of warm, merry energy, Shea was completely calming. Shaking her hand, Olivia felt like her heartbeat noticeably slowed. It wasn't that she seemed chilly, exactly, but there was definitely something a little distant about her.

"It's nice to meet you," she said, smiling.

"You'll do well here," Shea said kindly, as if she somehow knew. Maybe she did? Olivia was still trying to wrap her head around the idea of instinct.

Shea handed Olivia a bottle and one of the babies to feed, and gave her a few quiet instructions. It was the closest that Olivia got to resting that day, curled up in a rocking chair with an eagerly sucking infant.

There were games throughout the afternoon—sometimes organized events with stickers for prizes, but more often elaborate imaginative adventures of free play. Olivia was recruited as a patient, as a grocery shopper, and as a student, naming the letters that were presented to her. She understood only about one word in five, but the children didn't seem to expect more of her and Addison translated when it was necessary. She admired the tree that Oette was determined to show her over and over again.

The last sleepers, Lucy among them, were finally roused and drawn into the play. Lucy spent much of the last half of the day buried in Olivia's hair, chattering in her ear. Olivia understood her just about as well as a squirrel as she did when Lucy was a little girl.

Snack time was only shorter than lunch, not less chaotic.

Cherry had paperwork for Olivia that she signed as parents started filtering in to pick up their kids.

The parents themselves looked just like ordinary people; Olivia wasn't sure why she expected that they would look enchanted or magical—Ian and Lucy hadn't. Not one of them had animal ears or antlers, and they all wore modern Montana clothing; there wasn't a single swishing cloak or witch's hat. No wands poked from their purses or diaper bags.

They picked up their kids just like mundane parents, happy to see them and anxious to leave ("Tara, please hurry! The post office closes in ten minutes!"). They smiled at Olivia when they were introduced, and must have known she wasn't a shifter, but seemed to accept her presence without question.

Oh, but Cherry wasn't a shifter either, Olivia remembered, and she wondered how Cherry had gotten started in this business. Then she wondered how many of the parents were shifters, which brought her thoughts back to what Ian was. Some kind of shifter, for sure, but he'd made a point of saying that it was impolite to ask and he hadn't volunteered it. It must be something that shifters kept private when they could. There was, of course, a limit to how much they could hide in the day care.

And the whole point of the day care was to protect their secrets.

"I'll show you the clean-up routine," Addison said. Olivia wasn't sure how she still had so much energy; Olivia felt done-in after just half a work day. "How are you liking Tiny Paws so far? Are you new to Nickel City?"

The two of them had hit it off at once; there was something about being spit up on by the same baby that seemed to break down all the usual tensions of meeting new people.

Olivia liked everyone at Tiny Paws, right down to the squalliest baby. She had worked plenty of retail and food service, but this, from the very first, felt like a *meaningful* job, not a pay-the-bills and tolerate-the-management job. *Part of a team.* A lot of jobs said that but never really meant it.

Addison showed her where the cleaning supplies were and walked her through disinfecting the toys and hard surfaces. The bedding was all thrown into a washing machine and the mats were wiped down. The floor was vacuumed, and all of the toys returned to their bins except for what the final few children were playing with.

They talked as they went through the routine, straightening blocks and dollhouses. It turned out that Addison hadn't been in Nickel City that long, either, only a few months. They agreed that it seemed like a nice town, and that living out of suitcases was a drag.

"I spent nearly a month on the floor in my cousin Wendy's craft room," Addison said. "The housing market is so tight right now!"

"I'm mostly taking this job because the rent is so much higher than I expected," Olivia confessed. "I was hoping to get new furniture, but I'm thinking I'll have to shop Craigslist."

"We can go garage saling this weekend if you'd like," Addison said. "My boyfriend has a giant work truck we can use if you need to haul something."

"Oh, thank you," Olivia said. "I don't really know anyone here yet, except for my next-door neighbor, I-Ian. He's Lucy's dad." She cursed herself for tripping over his name. And of course Addison already knew that he was Lucy's dad. She felt her cheeks heat and hoped the blush didn't show.

Addison tilted her head, like she was trying to identify a weird smell. Was *she* a shifter? Olivia suddenly wondered. It must be a handy thing to just know, and not have to ask.

Lucy was playing now, carefully stacking blocks as high as she could get them, which wasn't very, because she kept putting small blocks on the bottom. Oette was sitting quietly nearby, patting the dirt around her sapling, and Gabby was a wolf puppy, chewing slowly on her tail like she was about to fall over into sleep at any moment.

"He's pretty cute," Addison said archly. "Ian, I mean." Then, delightedly, "You've got a crush on him!"

"Did instinct tell you that?" Olivia asked, before she could think that it might be a taboo topic, like asking what kind of shifter someone was. There was so much that she didn't know!

Addison laughed. "It didn't need to," she assured Olivia. "You're adorable. And Lucy already worships you, so you're halfway in."

Olivia stammered a half-hearted protest but she laughed with Addison. If she was a shifter, what kind would Addison be? A deer, maybe? Or a squirrel like Lucy? She had enough energy.

"I am here for Adoette!"

Olivia turned in alarm to find a strange woman standing in the center of the room. She was wearing a business suit and had gray hair slicked back from her face, which was drawn into a no-nonsense scowl. Olivia was quite sure that no one had buzzed this woman in.

Addison didn't seem the slightest bit surprised. "Oette! Your mother is here for you!"

Oette got to her feet, heaving the potted plant precariously up with her, and in a motion so fast that Olivia couldn't track it, the woman was across the day care crouching down beside her. But she wasn't looking at Oette, only Lucy.

"Bye!" Lucy said, waving at Oette. "Bye, Oette!"

Before Oette could respond, the woman was sweeping Oette and the plant up in her arms and jerking them away from Lucy. She stood and glared at Addison. "We will not be returning!" she declared.

Oette's face went from surprised to dismayed and in the time that it took her to screw up her face to protest, the two of them blinked out of sight with the sapling.

Olivia stared at the space where they'd been as Lucy, her face scrunched in confusion, gave a test sob. The little girl clearly wasn't sure if the situation warranted a full cry.

"Well," Addison said briskly. "I'll tell Cherry. There's a waiting list."

Olivia saved her questions until Addison returned, distracting Lucy by making faces at her until she laughed and went back to her blocks.

"Who...er...what...?" Did this fall into *rude to ask* territory?

"That was Isadora Larix. She's an elemental."

"A what?"

"A dryad, really. You know that big tree down by Belle Lake?"

The *big tree* was listed as a tourist attraction, which Olivia had thought was quaint and odd. She hadn't made a point of going to see it yet, not sure how exciting it would really be; Montana trees hadn't really impressed her so far. "I've heard of it."

"That's Isadora's tree. No one knows that much about her, but she's really old and really powerful. She's part of the reason there are so many shifters around here. She protects a lot of the forest nearby."

"Why did she just pull Oette out of day care?" Olivia asked. Lucy seemed to have forgotten about the little scene, but Olivia still remembered how Isadora had looked at the little girl, with alarm and mistrust.

"Who knows why that woman does anything," Addison said. "She's eccentric and unpredictable."

Olivia felt a little dizzy. What other magic was there in the world? She'd just barely gotten used to the idea of *shifters.*

Their phones buzzed in tandem with the security app alert and Addison glanced at her screen, then grinned devilishly at Olivia. "Oh look, it's Lucy's dad. You should have him take you out there to see the tree. It's open to the public every second Thursday. You know the check out procedures!" Then she thumbed open the door lock and swept Gabby into her arms to go out into the courtyard to avoid contaminating the playroom they had just cleaned, leaving Olivia alone with Lucy.

She wasn't sure why the little girl smelled faintly of sulfur and smoke, but she didn't worry about it long as she picked up Lucy and went to meet Ian.

CHAPTER 10

*J*an was not sure that anything in the world had ever looked as right as Olivia holding Lucy. They were talking quite seriously as they walked, Lucy nodding very gravely over some aspect of their conversation. Olivia knew he was there, but Lucy had not caught on yet and he had a moment of perfect joy watching the two of them converse.

Then Lucy caught sight of Ian at the doorway into the day care and gave a screech of joy, all but pitching herself out Olivia's arms in his direction.

Olivia gave a wincing smile and carried her to the gate. "Fingers and feet," she was reminding Lucy. It was the code phrase to remind young shifters to stay in human shape. Ian had to use it a lot taking Lucy shopping these days.

Today, he'd had the luxury of going to the grocery *all by himself*. It had taken him a fraction of the time it usually did to accomplish the basic task, with no car seat to wrestle, no sudden detours to the restroom, and no worrying that Lucy would suddenly turn into a squirrel. He'd been more able to concentrate on his shopping list than usual, not having to keep up a conversation that was half nonsense, and they didn't have to stop to count all the pictures of cows in the dairy section.

He only caught himself mooing at the cows once, when an old lady picking out cottage cheese gave him a concerned look and he realized what he'd done.

His hands brushed Olivia's as she handed Lucy over the colorful gate and Ian had a shiver of delight that had nothing to do with instinct; his dragon was soundly asleep. It was just the thrill of her skin against his, reminding him that it had been a long time since he'd had anyone but himself in a carnal way.

"Daddy! Daddy!" Lucy sang happily.

"How was the writing?" Olivia asked. "Did you get a lot done?"

Astonishingly, Ian thought that the question was genuine. She really did want to know how it went, and wasn't trying to imply that it was a useless waste of his time.

"Daddy! Daddy!" Lucy was on repeat and Ian bounced her to keep her entertained while he talked with Olivia.

"It's been great," he said honestly. "I mean, I still spend the first hour or so of every day absolutely sure that Lucy is getting into something, that I'm supposed to be watching her, checking over my shoulder every ten minutes. It took a little getting used to, but then I was able to actually dig down and write two whole chapters and a new outline for the second act. I figured out all the stuff that had been bogging me down the past four months and there was a villain that I didn't really have a motive for that—wow, this is a lot more than you wanted to know, sorry."

"No, it's awesome," Olivia said quickly. "You'll have to tell me more about it some time." Her smile was sincere, crinkling up the corners of her eyes.

There was a little pause and Ian suddenly wondered if that was meant to be an invitation to ask her out. It didn't help his concentration that Lucy was still saying, "Daddy, daddy, daddy!" at basically the top of her lungs.

Before he could muster a response, Olivia went on, reporting, "Lucy had a great day. She's in a new shirt because there was a yogurt accident at snack time. She slept about thirty minutes during quiet time."

"Ah good," Lucy agreed sagely.

"And you? How's the new job?" Ian asked. If she wasn't enjoying it, would she blame him for suggesting it?

But Olivia smiled like sunshine. "I am run off my feet," she said in a confessional voice, "and I was spit up on twice. I think that Gil put goldfish crackers in my socks, and I almost dropped a baby, but on the whole, it worked out really well."

"I'm glad to hear you aren't planning to flee screaming," Cherry said, suddenly appearing from behind them. "The first day can be a little intense. But the kids loved you, and you were a great help."

Ian told himself that Olivia's smiles weren't exclusive to him and it was silly to be jealous when she swung her grin to Cherry. "Thank you for the opportunity," she said sincerely.

"We're open at seven tomorrow," Cherry said. "Would you prefer a morning shift or the afternoon? We could also arrange for four tens if that was more amenable to your schedule."

"I am definitely not in shape for a ten-hour day of this," Olivia laughed.

Lucy was still saying, "Daddy, daddy, daddy!" but more insistently now, protesting the boredom of being held.

"Ready to go home, Chicken Little?" Ian asked her.

"Squill!" Lucy suggested.

"No squirrel," Ian told her firmly. "Fingers and feet!"

Lucy mumbled something that might have been *fingers and feet* or *feeble and sheets* or *eagerly sleet.*

Cherry and Olivia continued to talk quietly and Ian told himself that he wasn't really eavesdropping if he happened to be able to overhear them while he was putting Lucy's shoes on her wriggling feet.

Olivia opted for the morning schedule and Ian was disappointed. Drop-offs had proved much harder than pick-ups and he didn't want to scar Olivia with Lucy's clingy hysteria.

Lucy's shoes were on, and her bag was all packed up. He didn't have a reason to linger any longer.

He told himself that what he felt right now for Olivia was just attraction, clearly. His dragon was all but snoring in his head, so it couldn't be instinct that made him tingle in her direction. She was just…beautiful and funny and wonderful with Lucy, clearly capable and clever. It was just flesh, not fate, right?

He glanced at the gate into the day care and caught her standing there. She waved cheerfully and turned away. Had he caught her gawking after him? Maybe she had just happened to be lingering. Even if he was totally crushing on her, that didn't mean she was attracted to him, too.

Within him, as if his inner turmoil was noisy, his dragon stirred in his sleep.

Lucy was still saying, "Dad-dy, dad-dy," but it was a sing-song now, just noise that happened to fall into words.

Ian gathered her up with her bag and soothed his dragon back down into slumber.

He didn't have time or heart to spare pursuing romance, and just look at what had happened with his last relationship.

Being a dragon had ruined his marriage and destroyed his family.

CHAPTER 11

Garage sales in Nickel City were much the same as they'd been in Florida: very hit and miss.

"What is it?" Olivia asked Addison in an aside.

"I think it's a wine decanter?" Addison guessed. "But maybe a vase?"

Neither of them dared to touch it.

"Is it really…?"

"Two fucking deer on a crocodile, I think?" It was strange to hear Addison use dirty words after a week at the day care with both of them being careful of their language, and Olivia burst out laughing at the surprise of it.

"Does the artist realize that they are both bucks if they have antlers?" she asked.

"I'm sure there's a hot market for stylized gay animal art," Addison said, trying to smother her amusement. "It's only five dollars, I could get it for you as a housewarming gift if you like it."

"Please don't," Olivia begged. "Seltzer would probably break it and I'd have to pretend that I was sorry."

"Oh, you could do that Japanese ceramics thing that they do with broken porcelain, with the gold veins, you know?"

"Kintsugi," Olivia remembered from her vault of obscure facts and information. "And then I'd have a *fancy* fucking deer decanter I had to pretend to like. Let's see what she's selling that little end table for."

They left the driveway with a ten dollar table but left the decanter behind, still giggling over its absurdity.

They found a sturdy single bed frame and a mattress that was still in plastic at the next garage sale for a hundred dollars even, and wrangled them together into the back of Addison's boyfriend's pickup. Addison was stronger than she looked and Olivia wasn't going to be beat out by her. The end table fit in the crew cab, along with a blender from the next garage sale, and a pile of flowered plates to replace the set that had broken on her trip from Florida.

"Don't let me look at the books," Olivia said, and Addison steadfastly dragged her past them. "I have seven boxes of books and no bookcases yet."

They picked up a folding table and two chairs that would work for the kitchen, at least temporarily, but every couch and loveseat that they looked at smelled like cat pee or smoke.

"Not that everything doesn't smell a little like smoke right now," Addison said, squinting at the sky.

The sun was bright and the sky was clear of clouds, but there was a faint smell of woodsmoke to the air and every-thing was just a little hazy.

"Is it often like this?" Olivia wanted to know, before she remembered that Addison was not a long-time resident.

"Roderick says that it's not uncommon," she said with a shrug. "This year is maybe a little worse than usual."

"Is it dangerous?"

Addison shook her head. "Nah. Smoke travels a really long way; these fires are probably a hundred miles from here."

Addison tirelessly hit two more dead-end garage sales with her and then helped Olivia unload the truck back at her house. They drove in by the alley and carried the frame in the back door.

"This is cute!" Addison said kindly of the tiny house. "It's a darling neighborhood. Hot neighbor, too."

Olivia nearly dropped her half of the frame as she glanced to see if Ian was actually there. He was not, Addison was only teasing her, and Olivia had to laugh at herself as they maneuvered the bed to the bedroom. Seltzer did his best to stay underfoot and tolerated Addison cooing over him and scratching his ears.

"I'll get Roderick's tools and we can put this together," Addison offered when Seltzer had been given his due. "Because we are bright, capable, and independent adults."

"Would you like a drink?" Olivia offered. "Orange soda or white wine. I also have Kool-aid. Because we are bright, capable, and independent."

"Just soda," Addison said cheerily. "Whew! Does this place have air conditioning?"

"There's a ceiling fan," Olivia said, "but I haven't figured out how to turn it on."

She was gratified that Addison also could not find a switch or remote that controlled it.

"I'll have to call Veronica to see how to work it," she said, when they'd both been defeated.

"Veronica Chase?" Addison said in distaste.

"You know her?" Olivia said in surprise. It really was a small town.

"She's…kind of a thing here in Nickel City. Thinks of herself as a robber baron, bought a lot of property up at a good time and is milking the short term rental market. New legislation limiting rentals is probably the only reason you got a lease instead of a sky-high daily rate. She owns the Tiny Paws building, too, and she and Cherry are not exactly on warm terms. Watch out for her."

"Does she know…what kind of day care it is?" Olivia asked cautiously. Shifting didn't seem to be a thing that was spoken of at all.

Addison shook her head. "I can only imagine what Veronica would do with that information. Something horrible, blackmail maybe. She's a weasel."

"But not literally."

Addison gave a shout of laughter. "Not literally!" she agreed.

It was still amazing to Olivia that it *could* be literal.

They got the bed frame together with minimal effort, and set up the table and chairs in the kitchen. It almost looked like a home, despite the boxes that still lined the walls. "I'll keep my eyes out for bookcases and a couch," Addison told her. "That corner really could use an ugly fucking deer vase."

"We will not speak again of the banging bucks," Olivia said in mock-dire tones.

The only thing that had really been unpacked was Olivia's beloved camera and a few of her framed photographs, stacked on one of the unopened boxes.

"Oh, are you a photographer?" Addison asked.

It was an innocent question, and Olivia knew that it shouldn't cause as much pain as it did. "I…used to be."

Some day again, maybe she could pick up a camera

without feeling like it was weighted with a thousand little heartaches and betrayals.

Addison looked like she wanted to ask, but she backed off at the last moment. Olivia realized that she probably had frozen up rather obviously and forced a smile onto her face. "I imagine that's not a very welcome hobby in a society of secret shifters where a careless shot might betray them."

If Addison had any clue what a turmoil she had set off in Olivia's chest, she was happy to brush it under the rug and follow the offered topic. "It does complicate things sometimes," she agreed mildly. "Hard to get a safe family photo when the toddler has decided to be a giraffe full-time and senile Uncle Lenny the tiger is constantly photo-bombing things in stripes."

"Just your standard unexpected exotic pets," Olivia chuckled. "Don't mind the emu wearing dad's hat."

They laughed, but Olivia felt like the easy camaraderie that they'd had earlier was more strained now, just a little cool around the edges, and she couldn't help but wonder if it was her own fault.

"I should go," Addison said, in the same cheerful voice she used for preschoolers. "Roderick will fuss about his truck and I should take it back to him and let him kiss it and rub off the smudges with a soft cloth."

"Thank you so much for your help," Olivia said sincerely, and she wanted to thank Addison for her friendship, too, but she was too afraid to acknowledge it. If she did, she might lose it. "Can I give you gas money?"

Addison waved her off. "Of course not. This is what friends do."

Friends.

Olivia walked her to the back door, thanking her several more times until she probably sounded ridiculous and needy, and then had to chase Seltzer down when he tried to follow Addison to the truck and jump up into the cab with her.

He protested being held, but Olivia risked his claws to carry him back into the house, glancing next door.

"You've lost your outdoor privileges," she reminded him. "You can't go around catching baby squirrels in this town."

He growled and his fluffy tail lashed against her thigh.

CHAPTER 12

Olivia knew that Lucy had gotten out even before she heard Ian calling for her. "Lucy? Lucy!"

Seltzer was back in the tall grass by the fence between their yards, darting around after something in the weeds with only his tail really visible. Olivia didn't let him out by himself anymore. Although she was more and more sure as the days passed that Lucy would be safe with Seltzer, she was worried that he would be unable to resist his hunting instinct and might hurt the little girl before she could shift back to human form. It did help a lot that Lucy wasn't the slightest bit afraid of him and rarely ran away. They had played together enough, carefully supervised over the past few weeks, that they seemed to understand how to do it safely now. Olivia loved those moments, hanging out with Ian watching Lucy and Seltzer together, and she liked Ian more every time they talked.

Olivia was always ready with a squirt bottle in case things got out of hand, because she was pretty sure that "My cat ate your daughter" would put a heck of a damper on any romance that might be blooming between them.

She picked it up now. "I think she's over here!" she called, just as a squirrel darted her direction from the tall grass and climbed up onto the porch railing in a lightning fast move.

Seltzer dashed after, leaping to the railing as Lucy flung herself at Olivia.

Olivia handily caught Lucy and let her swarm up one arm to hide in her hair, shaking with squirrel laughter.

It was something she never expected to add to her resume, Olivia thought. She could now play the *trapeze* part of squirrel acrobatics.

Seltzer balanced on the railing, meowing and lashing his fluffy tail as he watched for an opportunity to follow Lucy. Olivia hissed at him, brandishing the hated bottle of doom, and Lucy chattered mockingly.

Seltzer settled back onto his haunches, his fur spilling off of either side of the rail, and turned his head to groom himself in offense, pretending that he'd never been interested in anything else.

Ian came up from beside the house, having bolted around to the end of the driveway. "Lucy," he said in surrender, coming up the porch steps. "Fingers and feet, remember?"

Lucy gave a tiny sigh and scrambled straight down Olivia's leg like gravity had no meaning, to pop into her little girl form. She was wearing a pink dress, but was barefoot.

"You remembered your clothes!" Ian exclaimed in joyful surprise. "Good job!"

"We've been practicing at Tiny Paws," Olivia said, and she was pretty sure she was smiling really foolishly. Ian's whole face was alight with delight and his happiness seemed to make her knees weirdly weak. "Well, Addison has been doing most of that," she felt compelled to add.

She wasn't a shifter, she reminded herself, and what she felt for Ian was probably just a silly crush.

But when they were smiling at each other on her porch, it felt like something more. She was sizzling with attraction, and she was pretty sure from his lingering gaze and the way he didn't seem to know what to do with his hands that he felt the same way.

She knew what she wanted him to do with those hands, that was for sure.

Lucy was standing on her tiptoes beside the porch railing and Seltzer was leaning off of it to sniff at her offered hand, puzzled.

"Sezzer!" she said eagerly. "Kitty!"

Seltzer flowed down to the deck and circled Lucy, to her delight, twining his tail after him. Lucy was toddler-rough with her petting but Seltzer didn't seem to mind.

"I think that Lucy confuses Seltzer," Olivia said, because she ought to say something, and most of what she could think of wasn't really appropriate in front of Lucy.

"I get that," Ian chuckled. "Lucy confuses me, too."

Lucy was crouched down in that effortless way that children could do because their knees were still flexible and they kept their muscles toned by running everywhere. Seltzer nearly knocked her down rubbing against her. He was purring now, and Olivia wasn't sure if he really liked the little girl or if he was just trying to convince her to turn back into a toy to chase.

Olivia gathered up her nerve. "Speaking of confusing," she said, before she could stop herself, "do you want to go out some time?"

There, she'd said it. There was no taking it back. She had wrestled back her doubts and committed.

"Are you asking me out on a date?" he asked in astonishment.

"I guess I am," Olivia said with an embarrassed chuckle. "I mean, I know you have a lot going on. I have a lot going on. There's…a lot going on." Was she giving him enough of an out? Too much? "You don't have to." Had she completely ruined the warm friendship that was growing between them by trying to make it into something more? She could have kicked herself, because as much as she wanted to tumble this guy in a pair of silk sheets, she liked him for a friend even more.

But Ian was smiling at her with sunshine in his face. "I love the idea. I'll get someone to watch Lucy some evening this week. Roderick owes me one. I'll take you out to dinner and we can do a few tourist things."

"It's the second Thursday of the month this week," Olivia said, because she'd been watching for the date on her calendar. "Addison suggested that you take me out to dinner and show me Isadora's tree."

Was it ridiculous to propose a date to see a magic tree? Or to point out that Addison was trying to set them up? Olivia hadn't second-guessed herself this much since she was in middle school as a student, all nervous and unsettled around boys.

But Ian wasn't just a *boy*. He was this gorgeous guy, an amazing dad, and he was a *shifter*. There was a whole world of magic that Olivia was just discovering, and he was like her door to it. Her gateway drug.

And he looked at her like she was the one who had enchanted him.

"That sounds great," Ian said, and if his ears were pink and his grin sort of foolishly broad, Olivia suspected that she looked exactly the same. "Oh, Lucy, leave the kitty. Too rough!"

Lucy was taking handfuls of Seltzer's fur and trying to pick him up. He gave a little growl of warning and squirmed from her grip to flee the porch. Ian intercepted Lucy when she ran to follow him, swinging her up into the air. She shouted with laughter and wrapped her arms around his neck. "Daddy!" she shrieked.

Then she gave Olivia a sideways look over Ian's arm. "Daddy and Owivee!"

Olivia's heart gave a little leap in her chest. It was just a date, she told herself. Just one date to see how things might go when they didn't have a proto-chaperone following them around trying to put dangerous things in her mouth and climb curtains.

But she really liked the sound of *Daddy and Owivee.*

CHAPTER 13

$\mathcal{I}$an thought that having Olivia work the early shift at Tiny Paws actually worked out pretty well.

It is amenable, his dragon agreed, but there was an undertone of impatience to its words. *She is ours. You should be more forward.*

That perversely made Ian want to take it slower.

But Lucy warmed up to her immediately and morning hand-offs quickly lost their terror. She still fussed a little about Ian leaving, but he and Olivia developed a sly routine where Olivia would hold Lucy, technically just so that Ian could hang up her bag and put her shoes away. He stretched out the simple task and then they would stand together and chat until Lucy started to get bored. Olivia would propose a game that she liked or remind her of a friend waiting in the day care and Ian suspected that Lucy didn't even notice when he finally slipped reluctantly away. He wasn't sure which one of them he wanted to leave less.

Sometimes Lucy would eye them suspiciously, like she knew that she was being had, but Olivia assured him that his daughter always had a fun time at the day care after he left.

"She spends some time on my shoulder every day," Olivia told him. "She wants to know stories about Seltzer, and I've worked up to understanding about one word in four!"

He cherished their morning conversations almost as much as he did their semi-regular evening playdates with her cat and his daughter.

Ian also wryly thought that he got considerably more socialization of his own now that he was seeing other parents at pick-up and drop-off. He hadn't realized exactly how isolated he'd gotten, working full-time from home and having to keep Lucy's prodigious shifting a secret.

Vivian, one of the nurses at a local clinic, had a lengthy conversation with him about food, reassuring him that feeding Lucy oven-baked chicken tenders five days a week wouldn't cause her any lasting harm. "Sometimes kids get really picky," she said with an understanding laugh. "Slip some vegetables in as you can, but calories are calories and you have to pick your battles." She rolled her eyes at Tara, who was very studiously—if unsuccessfully—trying to tie her own shoes. "Sometimes, it's just whatever they will eat. Your daughter certainly looks like she has plenty of energy."

(Lucy, at the time, had been running from end to end of the entryway, tripping over shoes and bouncing up with boundless gusto.)

A woman who introduced herself as Chloe had a little boy a bit younger than Lucy and she admitted to Ian that she hadn't even known about shifters until her son became one. "I mean, I knew he liked baths," she chuckled. "But I never expected him to turn into a *penguin.*"

In one of those "how small is this town?" moments, Ian

found out that Chloe was dating Clay, one of the Nanuk brothers and the oldest sibling of one of his best friends from high school. She was clearly still in the blushing-a-lot stage of the romance, and Ian found himself wondering if Olivia blushed when she talked about him.

What stage of romance were he and Olivia in? he wondered. Were they at any stage at all? Was there a "we're not really talking about the fact that we like each other but sometimes we can't meet each other's eyes and laugh really awkwardly" stage? How was he supposed to get past that to the "take all of her clothing off and make sweet love until we're both sweaty and spent" stage? It had been two weeks since they'd met and it simultaneously felt like a year and just a day.

One of the best parts of day care pickup was reconnecting with Roderick, one of his other high school friends. It seemed like the only times they managed to catch up anymore was when Ian had a plumbing problem. Ian recently had his daughter Gabby overnight with Lucy, which had given Ian at least five new gray hairs. Lucy was still begging him for more sleepovers, so at least one of them had enjoyed it.

"How's the writing going?" Roderick asked, the afternoon after Olivia finally asked him on a date.

Ian was never sure if his friends asked about his work because they cared about it or if they were just being polite.

Does it change your answer? his dragon asked pointedly. The prickly feedback feeling was distracting.

"Day care is the best invention since television," Ian admitted. "I've made more progress on my book in the last week than I have in the last seven months, since Lucy learned to walk and shift."

Roderick nodded in understanding. "I tried bringing

Gabby with me to a job once when I couldn't get a spot with Cherry—before she started Tiny Paws—and it was just a disaster from start to finish. And that was before she could shift! I thought I was going to get fired."

It was meant as a joke, because Roderick ran his own little one-man plumbing business.

Ian chuckled. "Speaking of trouble, would you be willing to watch Lucy on Thursday night?"

Roderick shrugged, tickling Gabby because she was getting restless. "Sure. Hot date with your book?"

"Maybe an *actual* hot date," Ian said. He didn't want to think too hard about Olivia because it had an embarrassing effect on his body. "With a real life *woman*."

Roderick whistled. Gabby immediately tried to mimic him, blowing fruitlessly through her pursed lips. "Who is it?"

"Olivia," Ian said. "She lives next door, works here now."

"Oh, we've met. She seems great and Gabby likes her," Roderick said. "I'd be happy to watch Lucy for you. I owe you for that sleepover." Gabby was still trying to whistle and getting frustrated with her raspberries.

"Thank you, I know it's a lot to ask," Ian said. He was already wondering if it was a good idea. "Lucy's a serious handful," he warned. As if to prove his point, Lucy pelted away from him and had to be chased down and sat back up on the bench again, giggling and dangling her legs.

"Gabby's shifting now, too," Roderick replied with a grin. He bounced his daughter on one arm. Gabby had realized that if she couldn't make her lips make the noise she wanted, she could at least growl while she was blowing, and she sounded like a tea pot starting to boil. "I get it."

"Gabby's a wolf, though," Ian pointed out. "She stays on the ground. Lucy can climb walls and hide in shoes."

Roderick mimed a knife to the heart. "Addison would be there," he reminded Ian. "You clearly don't trust *me*, but she knows how to handle Lucy."

How could this be worse than leaving her at the day care? Ian wondered. Why was he more worried about this?

You worry too much about everything, his dragon said with a huff.

Is that instinct? Ian wanted to know. *Or just your insufferable superiority?*

It's not instinct, his dragon offered impatiently. The dragon didn't deny its superiority. *You just spend too much time thinking about what people think of you. Our daughter is safe. We would know if she wouldn't be. You should have more confidence.*

Roderick was looking at him with a curious sideways look and Ian realized that he was scowling. "Is there a problem?"

Ian gestured towards his head. "Just getting a lot of extra advice in here," he said wryly. "You know how it is. Or maybe you don't. You don't have a dragon in your head."

Roderick chuckled and Gabby stopped kicking long enough for him to get a shoe onto her. "I do have a wolf," he reminded Ian. "And he's not a *tame* wolf."

Ian didn't want to argue with his best friend, but even a wild wolf was a world apart from a dragon.

I'm clearly better, his dragon sniffed.

"Have you told her?" Roderick asked.

Ian had to sort himself out from the conversation in his head and the struggle to get Lucy's shoes on. She was babbling at full volume and full speed. It was entirely nonsense, as far as Ian could tell. "Told who?"

"Olivia," Roderick said, like it was obvious. It probably was, if Ian could track a basic conversation.

Roderick lowered his voice. "She must know you're a

shifter since she's working here, but have you told her that you're a *dragon*?"

Not many people knew that there even *were* dragons. Shifters could recognize each other, but Ian had always been particularly careful about guarding the true secret of his nature. Telling Wanda about it had been a disaster that only reinforced his caution.

You did that wrong, his dragon said critically. *If you had listened to me…*

"I haven't told her yet," Ian said to Roderick. "I don't even know how serious we are. Or if there's anything to be serious *about.*" Lucy's shoes were on, so he let her loose to run laps in the entry with Gabby while he and Roderick gathered up the rest of their daughters' things.

His dragon made a noisy sigh of disgust in his head.

"Secrets are always trouble," Roderick reminded him. "And if she's the one…"

"I don't know if I believe in *the one,*" Ian said.

You don't think you are worthy of the one, his dragon corrected.

Can I have this conversation by myself? Ian asked in frustration.

Sorry, his dragon huffed. It did at least feel genuinely apologetic.

Roderick didn't seem to notice Ian's distraction; his face had taken on that soft look that he got when he talked about Gabby…and now Addison as well. "It's a real thing," he said. "It's not like a neon sign or a compulsion or anything. It's this feeling like…everything's perfect. Like, when you're in a hot tub and it's just the right temperature and the jets are in just the right places and you think your whole body is just going to melt in pleasure. And instinct is kind of humming, you know? Or it's like the soundtrack in a movie, where the music tells you that you're at the happy ending. It's like that when I look at her, or come home to her, or see her suddenly. There's *music*."

Instinct wasn't music for Ian, and it didn't hum. It burned, like the dragon it came with. It dragged him along like he had no free will of his own.

It wouldn't burn if you didn't fight it, his dragon reminded him. *Flow into it, don't run from it.*

"I don't know if it's like that for me," Ian said. He certainly liked Olivia, and he was full of nervous attraction for her. Sometimes it was hard to separate his dragon's bull-headed personality from the supernatural draw of instinct; he wasn't always sure when his dragon was insisting on something because it thought it knew better, and how much was that his dragon was interpreting instinct differently than Ian was.

I like Olivia, his dragon said unhelpfully. *I like her a lot.*

But is it instinct? Ian wanted to know.

Does it matter?

Did it?

"Thursday," Ian said sharply, noticing that Roderick was looking quizzically at him again. "Is Thursday okay? I was going to take Olivia to see Isadora's tree at Belle Lake."

Roderick was nodding his agreement. "That's a great idea," he said approvingly. "Thursday should work out fine, though we won't be able to take her overnight."

Gabby and Lucy were finally both ready to go. Ian and Roderick parted ways outside the front door, taking their respective daughters to their vehicles. Roderick had a giant crew cab truck for his business, Ian had a boring SUV that he'd picked for its safety rating and backseat space. He buckled Lucy into her car seat, reminded her that she was *never* to shift while they were driving (that had happened once and taken at least five years off of his life), and got into the driver's seat.

It suddenly occurred to him that he now had an official date scheduled. With Olivia.

Something inside of him vibrated with anticipation. He wasn't sure it was instinct, but as his dragon pointed out, did it matter?

"Big date tonight," Addison said to Olivia knowingly. "Tara, don't let Amy into the glitter, honey. She might try to eat it."

Amy, her bid for the tantalizingly sparkly forbidden fruit thwarted by the older girl, gave a squawk of outrage and turned into an owl, squirming from her clothing to beat her stubby wings against the legs of the table. Down floated around her like angry dandelion fluff.

Tara calmly nudged her out of the way with one foot.

"We're eating Chinese food and looking at a big tree," Olivia said. "I don't know if that's a date or a field trip."

Addison grinned at Olivia. "Depends on how it ends!"

Would Ian kiss her? Maybe it was a really *romantic* tree. Olivia knew it wouldn't be an overnight date, because it was a weekday, but maybe if they got to the good stuff really fast…? Not that they were doing *anything* really fast.

"Wear comfortable shoes," Addison warned her. "It's a bit of a hike."

The early afternoon went even more slowly than usual, despite a short crisis to chase down an escaped bird. It was a real bird, a parakeet from the little day care zoo, and its flight up into the rafters lit off a chaos of interest from the kids.

Amy shifted into an owl and beat her flightless wings with all her might, while Lucy immediately squirreled up, climbed the nearest wall, and started scrabbling across the actual ceiling. Jennifer turned into a puppy and howled and Gabby decided that must be the thing to do as well. Gil turned into an armadillo—forgetting all of his clothing —and rolled around in an anxious little ball.

"How is she doing that?" Olivia cried in panic, chasing in vain after Lucy. "What if she falls?"

Cherry, coming out from her office, calmly told her, "Squirrels can survive falling at their terminal velocity. She'd be fine. Lucy, honey, you're scaring the bird! Let's give him some space!"

It took a solid ten minutes that felt like at least an hour to coax Lucy back down and get the rest of the kids calm again and back in their clothing, while the bird continued to fly around in the open rafters. It finally came back when Shea, a baby in one arm, sat down in the rocking chair and began to sing.

It seemed unharmed by its adventure, and Cherry put it back in its cage and covered it with a cloth to let it recover in peace for a while.

Olivia wouldn't have minded being in a covered cage for a nap for a while, but the day continued to gallop along from minor crisis to minor crisis until it was time for her to go.

Lucy cried when she left, and tried to smuggle herself in Olivia's purse as a squirrel, forgetting about her fluffy tail.

Olivia had a few hours to shower the spit and sticky fingerprints off of herself, try three different hair styles (and finally opt for leaving it straight), and then fret about whether dating Ian would impede the cautiously flirty friendship that they'd developed. She wasn't good at friendships. She'd thought she was part of things before...and been wrong.

Olivia forgot to worry the moment that they met in his driveway and he gallantly held the car door open for her.

The Chinese restaurant was just a few blocks from Tiny Paws, and while Olivia had a moment of doubt eyeing the big grinning plastic dragon over the front door, it smelled amazing and the menu was mind-boggling.

"We get carryout a few times a month," Ian explained as he chivalrously held the door for her, "but I don't dare bring Lucy here to eat."

Olivia chuckled. "I can see why." The whole room was a perfect jungle gym for a squirrel, with lots of slatted dividers and waterfalls and dangling lanterns to climb up on.

"I'd have to coax her down off one of those lights and there'd be screaming when she fell in someone's soup, and they'd lose their business license and it would just be a disaster." It turned out that Ian, when not constantly distracted by a chattering toddler, was funny and charming and could carry on a coherent conversation. "We should get an appetizer, do you like spring rolls?"

Olivia was glad for the starter, because the rest of the order was quite slow, but she and Ian never seemed to run out of things to talk about. She quietly told him about Lucy's adventures on the ceiling. "I had no idea squirrels could do that."

Ian winced. "She can climb anything. Like almost literally anything. She's like Spider-Man."

"I was so scared she was going to fall," Olivia admitted.

"And can you even take a shifter to the hospital? That wasn't part of my day care training."

"It depends on what form she's in," Ian said gravely. "If she's a squirrel, I take her to the vet."

It took Olivia a moment to realize that he had dead-panned a joke at her and she nearly fell out of her chair laughing.

"Seriously," he said, when they'd managed to stop giggling, "even knowing that she could survive any fall, Lucy stops my heart twice a day at least. Don't think I don't appreciate what you guys at Tiny Paws are putting up with."

The way he said it, warmly, made Olivia flush with happiness. "I can't take a lot of credit for it," she said shyly. "I'm mostly a warm body to change diapers and wipe faces. Addison and Cherry are the ones who know what to do."

"You're much more than a warm body," Ian said, and it was just suggestive enough that Olivia's flush went nuclear.

The server came then, took their empty appetizer plate, and refilled water glasses.

"How are you liking Nickel City?" Ian asked neutrally, when the waiter was gone.

"It's not what I expected," Olivia admitted.

"In what way?"

"Well, I was expecting...a city." They both laughed and Olivia went on. "I read up on it, so I knew it was an old mining town, and I guess I knew that it would be quaint and small, but I didn't expect..." Olivia glanced around at the nearby tables.

"Shifters," Ian guessed quietly.

"It's like a fairy tale," Olivia admitted, and it was one of those moments where she had trouble meeting Ian's eyes. Sometimes, they seemed intensely gold and they made it hard to breathe. This was a fairy tale, and he was her prince.

To her delight, Ian reached across the table for her hand then, and held it until their food was served.

"Oh, I might have made a mistake eating that many spring rolls," Olivia said, when her enormous platter of surprisingly authentic Chinese food was finally served. She dug in with gusto, and for a while, their conversation was centered around enjoying the meal.

As they finished, Ian bemoaned the fact that he was going to have to plan a party for Lucy's looming second birthday. "I got away with not having to do anything for her first birthday," he explained. "But now she knows what a birthday party is, and she's been making me tell her how many days away hers is for weeks now. I still need to rent a bouncy house or something."

Olivia paid for the meal only because Ian got a text from Roderick with a photograph of Lucy and Gabby exactly when the bill came. Olivia thought he might insist on paying anyway, and there was a moment of testing each other before he finally said, "I'll let you get this one if you promise to let me get the next one."

She was very happy that they were both already thinking about a *next one.*

Then they drove to the forest reserve at the south shore of Belle Lake.

The walk out to the tree might have been romantic, deep in twilight, if it weren't for the fact that they were passing other visitors every few minutes. The trail was wide enough for two, but not for more, so while they held hands when they could, they were constantly having to go single-file, and it was easier to let go of him altogether rather than try to crane to keep contact like some of the other people were doing.

And the tree itself was everything that had been promised.

"I can't even see the top," Olivia said, craning her neck. There was a plaque near the base of the tree, and several people were snapping photos of it. A couple of people were touching the trunk, spreading their arms to get a sense of how monstrous the tree actually was.

Suddenly there was a woman with a wild mane of gray hair standing near them facing Ian, blazing anger in her face. She was dressed in authentic-looking Native American leathers, though her features didn't seem particularly Native and her eyes were bright green. Was she part of an educational demonstration? Her hands were balled into fists and she was glaring at Ian. "You're not welcome here," she hissed, stepping forward. "Get out of my forest." It certainly didn't feel like an act, and Olivia thought that if it was, it was in very poor taste. She looked very familiar, but Olivia couldn't place her.

Ian seemed as surprised by her advance as Olivia was and backed away with his hands spread. "I'm sorry," he said. "You're Isadora Larix. I don't think we've…met?"

She looked nothing like the last time Olivia had seen her.

"You're dangerous," Isadora snarled, and Ian actively flinched. "Get out."

They were starting to draw the attention of the tourists around them and Olivia was aware of the phones that were facing their direction. Some people were trying to discreetly snap pictures, sure a fight was about to break out. Others were overtly filming them.

Olivia wanted to take Ian's hand in solidarity, but hesitated. It was a first date, it would be a heck of an overreach to assume that kind of thing, especially in public, with all these eyes on them.

Ian glanced around at their avid audience and spread his hands in a peaceful gesture. "We'll go," he promised. "I'm...sorry?"

Isadora seemed to accept that, but Olivia was keenly aware of her gaze on them as they turned back the way they'd come.

"What was that about?" Olivia asked, when they were alone for a moment on the trail.

"I don't know exactly," Ian said hesitantly. He glanced behind them. "She's an earth elemental. I wonder if the forest fires are making her uneasy."

"I think I would call that hostile, rather than uneasy," Olivia said wryly. "Why would she think *you* were dangerous?"

Ian opened his mouth and then snapped it closed again.

Olivia was no dummy. She knew that Ian was keeping a lot of the details to himself, deliberately choosing not to tell her something about the angry woman...and about himself. Why would Isadora think he was dangerous? Ian was the nicest, sweetest guy she'd ever met. He was an absolute cupcake with his daughter.

It was frustrating, being at the edge of secrets like she was. She already knew that he was a shifter, if not what kind, and she knew about his adorable, squirrel-shifting daughter. It was like he'd introduced her to an entire five-story department store of magic and enchantment, but only allowed her access into the ground floor lobby.

Olivia told herself that it made sense not to share everything with her. Even with that magical instinct, how could he know that she was a good person who wouldn't blab his secrets? He had a little girl to protect, not just himself. Honestly, there was a whole world he was protecting.

The walk from the tree was much more subdued than their journey there. It was less crowded now, but they felt much less like talking.

They drove back to Nickel City making awkward conversation about things that neither of them were really thinking about. There was a series of unfortunately romantic songs on the radio, but it didn't really crack the tension.

Ian pulled into the back alley and into his own driveway, then made a show of smacking himself on the forehead. "I should have driven you home first," he joked.

"I think I can walk from here," Olivia chuckled, glad for a safe topic at last. "I wore comfortable shoes."

They got out of the car and Ian walked her to the place where their back fences joined.

Was he going to invite her in?

"I'm really sorry that didn't…go better," Ian said.

Olivia was quick to say, "I had a really good time, except for the crazy lady yelling at you." And the part where he wouldn't tell her *why*. But she didn't want to make the evening worse than it was with accusations of secrecy.

Ian dragged his hand reflexively through his hair, demonstrating why it often looked a little wild. "Yeah, that's the part I'm most sorry about," he said with a sheepish grin. "Can we try this again some time? Without the crazy yelling?"

Olivia thought about how nice and casual the dinner had been, and how cute and funny and kind Ian was.

"I'd like that," she said honestly.

"Olivia…" Was he going to shake her hand or maybe talk about the weather?

Just as Olivia thought she might have to initiate a kiss as well as a date, Ian took a step closer and put his lips to hers.

His confident touch more than made up for any weirdness on the date, starting firm and basic but quickly progressing to a deeper, more demanding kiss. He didn't wait for permission before he was pulling her close up against him, parting her lips with his tongue.

Not that Olivia was exactly protesting, opening her mouth eagerly and wrapping her arms around his neck.

He felt so strong and sexy against her, and his kiss was an exquisite mix of gentle and fierce. They crashed into the back fence and Olivia had only a moment to worry for splinters before she was distracted by his hand squeezing her ass and his kiss trailing down her neck towards the cleavage she had worried was too much. Now it seemed like hardly enough, because she wanted his touch everywhere and all at once. His other hand cupped one breast and he paused.

Was he waiting for a go-ahead? Giving her a chance to protest? Olivia made an impatient whimper of need and clawed at his shoulders, kissing his ear as the nearest target.

She had a moment of wonder. How far were they going to go? Was she ready to sleep with this guy? Was this the tipping point? What did they even have *time* for?

A shrill alarm cut the air and Ian cursed and pulled away, scrambling for his pocket. It didn't sound like his usual ringtone.

"Sorry, I set an alarm," he said. "For picking up Lucy."

"You thought you might forget her?" Olivia teased. Her lips felt the wrong size, tender and sensitive from his rough kisses, and they were still hungry. She was leaning up against the fence with no care at all about its rough surface.

"I thought I might get *distracted*," Ian said. "By you." Olivia hadn't known that sensible could be so sexy.

He closed the distance between their mouths again for one last, lingering kiss. "I'm sorry we don't have any longer."

"It is a work night," Olivia agreed breathlessly, disappointed but alive with anticipation. This was the next step she'd been hoping for. This and more…

She could be patient a little bit longer, she told herself.

But she hoped that it wasn't too much longer. She was starting to feel like a nun.

CHAPTER 15

Ian turned into Roderick's driveway and put the SUV into park, taking a moment to lean forward on his steering wheel and pull his thoughts together.

Roderick was going to want to know how the date had gone, and Ian didn't have an easy answer for him, any more than he did for his dragon.

Ian thought that the date with Olivia had suffered a few awkward moments—like the crazy woman who'd accused him of being dangerous—but it had at least ended on the right note, with a kiss so hot and ready that Ian got hard every time he remembered it. She was everything he'd imagined, willing and eager against his whole body.

She was so…

For a writer, Ian was at a complete loss for words when it came to describing Olivia. He could praise her beauty, her sexy grace, her clever turn of phrase, the sparkle of her eyes…and all of it fell achingly short of all the parts and pieces of her perfection.

Why even try to box her in with words? his dragon scoffed.

She is ours, and right, and that is all we need to know. You're always trying to describe and define things when they don't need to be.

Ian had a lot of writing critics.

His editor didn't pull punches. Wanda had stopped pretending to like anything he wrote pretty early in their relationship. "It's probably not bad," she would say, when she still tried to be kind, "but it's not my *thing*, you know?" And more than one review, before he learned not to read them, had scathing criticism of his plot, his characters, and the horse he rode in on.

But his very closest critic was the dragon who shared his head. It wasn't that the dragon didn't like Ian's writing, it was that it didn't see the point of writing at all. Writing didn't create wealth, or a tangible product, and it felt that the entire art was limiting and constrained…rather like the rest of Ian's mortal shell. Ian sometimes thought that his dragon didn't know how to *imagine*.

Ian could see into his dragon's heart and knew that it didn't mean to be as condescending as it was, and that part of the problem was that the dragon saw all the horrible, ugly drafts of the book as Ian created them in his head, unable to separate the creative process from the final product.

He had given up very early in trying to share the joy that he got from a singing phrase or perfectly conveyed feeling, and it was generally easier to write while his dragon slumbered.

It's not that I need to describe Olivia, he explained to his dragon, trying not to be impatient. *It's more that I **want** to write words that do justice to who and what she is, how she makes me feel.*

We are meant to be together, his dragon said, and Ian had a sense of a dismissive shrug. *Who cares about the rest. I don't understand why we aren't together **now**.*

Maybe she's the one, Ian agreed, gritting his teeth. *That doesn't mean I can drop all the important parts of my life to go lay her down in her backyard and make love to her. I have responsibilities.*

Such as getting out of the car he was parked in to collect his difficult and darling daughter from a very tolerant friend before she managed to chew through all of his electric cables or knock over a priceless vase because nothing was too high to be safe from her destruction.

Ian's dragon subsided with a grumble.

Sure enough, Roderick opened the door and immediately asked, "How was the date?"

"It was…*great.*" At that moment, all Ian could remember was how Olivia felt kissing him, the taste of her, the primal fire in his veins.

"Hi Ian! How's Olivia?" Addison called knowingly from the kitchen. "Lucy, your dad is here!"

"Daddy!"

Lucy was human, and dressed, which was more than Ian had honestly expected, and her face was purple with blueberries. Addison caught her with a washcloth, getting an expert swipe at the berry mess as Lucy streaked past her.

Gabby followed, rather clumsier, and offended that she was being left behind. She was as covered in blueberries as Lucy, but it wasn't as obvious against her mahogany brown skin.

"Gabby's walking!" Ian observed, intercepting Lucy to lift her up into his arms, mindless of the blueberries he was going to wear as she happily leaned her face into him and squeezed him with her tiny arms.

"Not walking," Roderick said in despair. "No walking. Only running."

"And shifting!" Addison sang. "How good is Gabby at shifting?"

"Abby! Ood!" Gabby cried.

Lucy responded, "I had ebeddy an sez I had gibber labor flubber wicket niddle!"

Ian honestly didn't understand a word of it, but she was very excited.

"They're really wound up," Roderick warned. "We've been medicating with blueberries."

"Sorry to keep you guys up late," Ian said, feeling guilty.

"Oh, no worries," Addison assured him. "It's not that late, and they had so much fun! I bet they both sleep like logs."

Lucy was going on enthusiastically, occasionally patting Ian on the side of the face to make sure he was paying attention to her as he gathered up her bag and accounted for the articles of clothing she'd come with.

"I owe you," he told Roderick.

"I'm not sure we're even for the sleepover yet," Roderick replied.

That was when Gabby realized that Lucy was going to leave and began to wail, in that thin, exhausted way that only an overstimulated child sensing defeat could manage. Addison swept up behind her, tickling and tipping her over upside down. Gabby tried not to laugh and Lucy recognized at this moment that she was the one leaving and started to cry as well.

That hastened the rest of their goodbyes and Ian took a struggling Lucy out to strap her into her carseat. "Fingers and feet," he reminded her, buckling her in. "Fingers and feet."

Lucy looked at him solemnly through her tears. "Fimber an wheat," she agreed reluctantly.

"It's important," Ian reminded her intensely.

Lucy's lower lip trembled and she stuck her fingers in her mouth, nodding.

His dragon was simmering, not asleep, and Lucy was exhausted, but not to the point of a fit. Instinct didn't tell him to wait, so Ian guessed that she would stick with her human form long enough to get home. Ian gave her a kiss on the forehead and tucked one of the car's back-up stuffed animals into the carseat with her.

By the time he got home, Lucy was asleep, boneless and sweet with her lashes over her cheeks. Ian carried her carefully inside and decided to leave her in her day time clothes to sleep, taking off only her shoes. There was a chance of an accident, but the risk of waking her up while he changed her and then having to try to get her back to sleep after a short nap was more horrifying.

There were still lights on in Olivia's house and Ian gazed over at it longingly. She wasn't in the kitchen. He wished that he dared to have her over, or dared to leave Lucy and go over to see if she was interested in continuing where they'd left off.

Even his dragon recognized that this wasn't an option. Their duty was to their daughter.

Instinct wasn't really helping, searing him without direction or purpose. *Be with her* was hugely unspecific, and it didn't really take into account that she had a job, and so did he, plus a daughter that needed his constant attention.

And Ian remembered too well what Isadora had said to him.

He was *dangerous.*

CHAPTER 16

They didn't talk about the kiss the next day, but Olivia knew they both remembered it well.

She especially remembered it when he dropped off Lucy and their hands brushed each other, both of them slowing to savor the touch.

His skin was pale enough for his blush to show, and she caught him adjusting himself uncomfortably, unable to keep her gaze from falling to his pants.

But as tempting as it was, she could not just vault the gate and leave Lucy behind with Addison to go have hot sex in his car, so they kept it all *very professional* and their conversation was the smallest talk that had ever been talked.

"All of Lucy's things are in her bag." Because they were every day.

"Oh good. We have fresh salt dough today. It's pink." Pink like Ian's cheeks, and probably Olivia's, too.

"Nice weather," Ian said agreeably.

"We'll probably play outside."

He finally left, and Olivia twirled with Lucy back into

the playroom and wrinkled her face when Addison made a kissy mouth at her.

The day went swiftly. Working at the day care didn't come with a lot of down time and Olivia didn't even check her phone until it was time to gather up her things and sneak out before any of the children could realize she was going.

Ian's car was gone from the back driveway when she got home and Olivia told herself that she wasn't his keeper —there were plenty of places he could be and none of them were any of her business.

Saturday was a mandatory middle school social, and it dawned bright and sunny, like all of the days since Olivia had moved there. She'd never lived anywhere so relentlessly comfortable. The heat wasn't intolerable, even if some people complained that they needed rain. Olivia was happy to have respite from the summer humidity that she'd left behind what seemed like a lifetime ago now.

"How do you like Nickel City?" one of her new coworkers asked.

Olivia had to bite back a quip about how it was unexpectedly full of magic and she wondered exactly how many of them knew about the little town's secrets. "It's really nice," she said agreeable. "A lot of trees."

She assessed them all as potentially shifters, and potentially friends, and thought with relief that she might enjoy her middle school job as much as she loved working at Tiny Paws.

She would probably come home with a lot less fur and down on her clothing.

The next day, she was puttering around in the overgrown backyard with Seltzer when she heard Lucy shriek in recognition. "Sezzer! Sezzer!"

"Fingers and feet!" Ian reminded her, coming to his back door and waving at Olivia.

She waved shyly back.

"Play wi Sezzer!" Lucy was insisting. "Play wi Sezzer."

She all but dragged Ian back around the fence. "I hope you don't mind company!" Ian called as they made their way around.

"Come into my garden, said the spider to the fly!" Olivia said, telling herself that there was really nothing dirty about the invitation. She felt several degrees hotter than she had just a moment before, and she was pretty sure that the sun wasn't beating any harder.

Seltzer stalked to greet Ian and Lucy at the back property line, pausing to sniff at each of them before leading them imperiously to Olivia.

"I have lawn chairs now," she said, showing them off. "Addison and I went garage saling this morning while the picking was good. I still have no couch or bookshelves, but I can entertain in my backyard now."

"Sorry to hear you've had difficulties finding a couch," Ian said, testing the very classic seventies-style lawn chair gingerly with his weight. "You could always take these inside for guests."

"I'll call it lawn chic!" Olivia agreed merrily. "It will start a home decorating revolution."

Lucy was engrossed with Seltzer, who was happy to play with her, chasing long pieces of grass and exploring through the overgrown garden.

"Can I get you a drink?" Olivia asked.

"Just water," Ian said.

Olivia went inside alone, understanding why he would

want to keep a careful eye on Lucy and the cat that could eat her if she decided to shift.

She had impulsively picked up a sippy cup for Lucy at one of the garage sales and she filled it with cool water and ice cubes, then carried all three drinks back outside.

Lucy rattled the ice cubes in her new cup, but seemed otherwise unimpressed. Ian prompted her to say thank you, which she eventually did, but she abandoned it quickly in favor of playing with the cat.

Ian was considerably more grateful, and Olivia was pretty sure that the way his hand brushed hers was not accidental. She was even more sure when she settled into the lawn chair next to him and he caught her hand in his. It was so natural to let their fingers twine together.

At first they just talked about Lucy, the weather, Seltzer. Ian was easy to talk to, familiar by now, and the conversation spilled into their past. He was watching Lucy out of the corner of his eyes but looking at Olivia, a trick that Olivia was perfecting herself after a few weeks at the day care.

"Who is Lucy's mother?" Olivia finally felt brave enough to ask, and she was glad that Ian didn't pull his hand away. Lucy was far enough away that she didn't hear the question.

"Her name is Wanda," Ian said. "She is a squirrel shifter from a great big family of them. A whole extended mess of cousins and aunts, all of them super into contact sports."

"Oh, lord," Olivia said in tones of horror.

"I shouldn't speak poorly of her, or her family," Ian said reluctantly. He was a good guy. A respectful guy. Olivia liked that about him.

"Not to Lucy, maybe," Olivia agreed, "but *contact sports.* You don't seem the type."

Ian laughed hard enough that Lucy came over to see what was up. She found her water cup and wandered back to where Seltzer was doing his perimeter march of the wooden back fence where Ian had kissed her after their date.

When she was out of easy earshot again, Ian went on. "Wanda and I met in college, and she seemed interesting and full of energy and I thought that's what I wanted. We dated for a while and got married, but it…sort of fell apart when Lucy was still a baby. Wanda didn't exactly appreciate finding out I was a—"

Olivia realized she was holding her breath. Was Ian going to tell her what he was? She was dying to know but didn't dare risk asking. She knew Addison was a lynx shifter because she often shifted at Tiny Paws, and she guessed that Roderick was a wolf because Gabby was, but she still didn't know what Shea was, or half of the parents she'd become friendly with.

But Ian seemed to reconsider what he was going to say.

"I sometimes wonder if she didn't date me for my family's money," Ian confessed. "I think she thought that I was a trust bunny, at one point."

"You're rich?" Olivia tried not to look skeptically at his house. He seemed more the type that was barely scraping by, with his very basic SUV and plain clothing.

Ian laughed. "No. Not at all. But my mother came from money, and Wanda knew that."

He was thoughtful. "I honestly don't wish her ill, but we really didn't suit each other well. She's ferociously extroverted and wanted constant interaction and excitement and, well, you've met me. I'm not the most stimulating company in the world."

"I think you're underselling yourself," Olivia told him. "I find you plenty stimulating." She blushed to hear the words from her mouth and worried that it would make things weird.

It didn't.

Ian gave her a hot-geek sideways smile and went on. "Our divorce was pretty amicable as these things go. She found a new guy right away, he's got a couple of kids, they're talking about getting married and having more. She seems…happy."

"It's not your fault, you know," Olivia pointed out. "Sometimes people just aren't meant to be together."

"And sometimes, they are," Ian added quietly.

Did he mean that as pointedly as it had come out? He'd mentioned instinct when they first met, and Olivia couldn't deny that there had been immediate sizzle. She really wanted to see how far that sizzle would go, and she was pretty sure that Ian did, too.

"Addison said you're a photographer," he said suddenly.

"I…sort of?" She glanced at him. His expression suggested that he was asking cautiously, but genuinely interested. "It's complicated."

"It's okay if it's just a hobby," Ian said. "I'd never judge."

"I thought I was going to make a career," Olivia said, hating the sour feeling at the pit of her stomach, dredged up by the past. "There was this group in Crescent City that I was…a part of, sort of. I mean, I thought I was a part of it, but I guess I really wasn't."

His fingers gave hers a little squeeze. The way the lawn chairs were set up, it was starting to cut off the circulation in her wrists to hold hands and Olivia wondered if it was too forward to scoot her chair closer to his so it was more comfortable.

She was delighted when Ian did it first, and their fingers twined together where the armrests touched.

He was remarkably easy to talk with, and since Lucy was still thoroughly occupied with Seltzer and some old plastic pots, Olivia told him about the co-op.

"It was supposed to be a community of photographers. We were going to go in together for some retail space, teach workshops, host shows, share opportunities for weddings and things. I did a lot of work for them—volunteer work. I built us a webpage, and did a bunch of fundraising, designed a lot of promotional stuff. I did all of the legwork to find a good location and organized the non-profit paperwork."

Olivia wasn't looking at Ian anymore. She wasn't looking at Lucy, either. She was just looking through her yard at her past.

"The woman leading this group, her name was Sunny. She was really beautiful and passionate and bohemian and I fell madly in love with her. I'd never been so happy. I was part of this amazing group of artists, and I got to be a part of making this amazing project happen."

She lapsed into quiet and Ian made little encouraging circles on the back of her hand with his thumb.

"I thought I was important," Olivia said, trying, like she always did, to keep her grief and hurt in proportion. "I thought I was important to the project and important to Sunny, and I wasn't. We hooked up on a road trip to look at a rental space in Orlando, but when we got back, she totally ghosted me. I thought the project had just died and we'd all drifted apart because we all had other careers and busy lives…but Sunny took the people she wanted to work with, behind my back and with all of my work, and started it up completely new. I never would have known if I hadn't randomly come across their gallery in a mall a year later."

Her hand had curled into a fist while she talked, and she remembered the sting of seeing all of their names on the door to the shop, in the fonts that she'd picked out for them, using the slogan and graphics that she'd designed. None of them had bothered to tell her the project was still on. None of them had been very good friends at all.

All she had wanted was to belong to something, be *part of a team,* and they'd shut her out. She'd never been sure if it was because she wasn't a good enough photographer for them, if they didn't like her, if Sunny had poisoned them against her because trying to make their relationship romantic had soured their friendship…

Ian was quiet. Was he dismayed because she was bi? Olivia worried suddenly. He didn't seem like the type to be bothered, but bigots weren't always obvious about it. His hand was still curved around hers and it felt very hot in the sun.

He was gazing out across the yard to where Lucy was following Seltzer around and Olivia had done almost all of the talking. She felt like an idiot, about the whole project, about telling him the story at all. They were at the holding hands stage of whatever they had, not the 'let me tell you about all my insecurities' stage.

Olivia opened her mouth to apologize for being a sensitive twit and grossly over-sharing.

"She broke your heart and stole your dream," Ian growled.

For a moment, his eyes were very bright and golden and angry and Olivia suddenly wondered what he might do, if Sunny were here in front of them now.

"It was a long time ago," Olivia said, forcing her hand to relax.

"She hurt you," Ian said without forgiveness.

It was easy to think of Ian as a big softy. He was gentle

with his daughter, and kind and respectful. These were things that Olivia liked about him. But she thought now that there was a core of steel to him, a fierce, protective strength that he tried to hide behind his easy-going manners and self-deprecation. *You're dangerous*, Isadora Larix had said.

Maybe he was.

But Olivia wasn't afraid of him, only excited by him.

Olivia found that her ex, and her broken dreams, didn't seem all that important any more. It had hurt so badly to be shut out, and she'd dragged around her fears of exclusion and inadequacy for so long that it felt weird to let them go. But she'd found a new place to belong, an amazing community of magic and enchantment that made the co-op look boring and mundane.

She almost laughed, to think of how much better this life was than the one that she'd idealized before. But it wasn't laughter on her lips when Ian leaned towards her, it was anticipation—

"Daddy, I have to go potty!"

Lucy was doing the *gotta-go-now* dance, abandoning Seltzer for the first time since they'd come over.

Ian drew himself up out of the lawn chair like a shot. "Sorry," he said. "When we gotta go, we gotta go."

Olivia had learned more about potty training in the past several weeks than she ever wanted to, and she stood to wave them away. "Bye, Lucy," she called. "I hope you'll come back later!" *Soon*, she wished. *Really soon.*

"It's almost nap time," Ian said regretfully, looking over his shoulder. "Maybe…tomorrow?"

But tomorrow was Monday, and the start of Olivia's last week at Tiny Paws. As much as she wanted to play hooky and see how gentle—or maybe *not* gentle—Ian was in bed, they both had duties and responsibilities.

It wasn't so bad, Olivia thought, when they'd disappeared into Ian's house. They didn't have to rush anything. She could just hear Lucy's protests as they went through the *I-don't-want-a-nap* routine.

Ian was the kind of guy worth waiting for.

She just hoped it wouldn't be too much longer.

CHAPTER 17

Ian felt like he'd spent the better part of the past year caught up in a game of two-person hide and seek where he didn't know the rules and the other player could turn themself invisible. It had been a long week, full of near-misses with trying to kiss Olivia again, and Lucy was so fractious that Ian suspected she was working on a new tooth.

"Lucy? Lu? Honey? I know you don't want to go to bed, but sometimes we have to do things we don't want to do."

Most of the time, Lucy was an amazing daughter and being a dad was the most rewarding thing that had ever happened to Ian. She was cute and clever and sweet, and Ian loved watching her grow and discover herself more than anything else in the whole world.

And yes, she had flooded the bathroom twice now and broken his last laptop and given him a handful of gray hairs and he couldn't open his cabinets without two free hands and a lot of cursing in a bid to keep her out of them. She was expensive and time-consuming and distracting from his career.

But she was worth every hassle and heartache, he told himself, and he told himself that twice as hard when he finally caught Lucy in his hands as she tried to leap over his head for the narrow space above the cabinet in the bathroom where he wouldn't be able to reach her.

"You have to go to bed now," he told her firmly. "You are wound up to eleven and I'm taking you to Tiny Paws early and if you don't have enough sleep you'll be cranky for Olivia's last day before middle school starts and you don't want that now, do you? I'll read your favorite book and you can put on your unicorn jammies and I'll turn on your sparkle sky night light, but you are going to bed now."

Dinner had run late, and there had been chaos in the bath when Lucy managed to get all of the towels in with her while Ian's back was turned, which is why the dryer was doing its noisy death rattle on top of everything else.

But they were past the tipping point from sleepy to strung out now. Lucy was absolutely punch drunk and shrieking with what started as laughter and ended as outrage when she realized that Ian wasn't interested in prolonging their game and was fully prepared to haul her to bed in either form.

Ian could pinpoint the moment where her brain completely checked out in exhaustion and she fell into an all-out fit.

Ian smelled smoke and sulfur, and made himself calm down, helplessly working through his toolbox of tricks for keeping himself from losing control of his dragon skills, at the same time he was trying to calm Lucy.

He tried singing to her, gently winding her back around in his arms in first little girl form and then in squirrel.

She'd gotten good at shifting with her clothing, thanks to Tiny Paws, so at least her clothing gave him some purchase when she was a little girl.

He tried rocking her, while she kicked and beat at him, and cupped her gently but firmly in his hands when she tried to squirm away as a squirrel. She didn't bite, but she did scratch him in her efforts to escape.

He tried scolding her, and reciting her favorite book, and she stubbornly remained a squirrel, scrabbling at his fingers and trying to squeeze herself through every tiny gap.

She was just so tired and worn out and overwrought and Ian felt so awful for her that he couldn't be impatient, even though he was probably more exhausted than she was by now.

"It's time for sleeping, Lucy. Time to close your eyes and go to bed so we can wake up happy. Dream time! Sleep time! Sweet, sweet sleep!" Ian babbled like she sometimes did, random words and sentence fragments. It was lucky he could string any adult words together in a row, anymore.

Lucy didn't calm down.

Instead, she chattered and scolded and at last she squeezed her tiny head through his thumbs and blew an unexpected jet of fire at him.

Ian let go of her in astonishment and caught her just before she reached the floor. He reminded himself that she couldn't hurt herself falling—squirrels could fall at terminal velocity and walk away—because it was easier to think about that than the fact that she had just *flamed* at him.

She was as surprised as he was, and Ian suddenly recognized that half of the random smoky smells around the house had been *her*, not the distant forest fires, and not *himself*. He wasn't sure if he felt relieved to know, or just appalled.

He was definitely shocked.

After a moment of frozen dismay, Lucy flung herself from Ian's cupped hands and raced for the window. As Ian shook himself to follow her, the bottom of the curtain caught on fire, and he could hear her scrambling up the wall behind it, squeaking as she went.

"Lucy! It's okay, Lucy!"

But was it?

Ian slapped directly at the flame, trying to smother it with his bare hands. Should he rouse his dragon? He wasn't sure what help he could be. Shifting to dragon form seemed less than useful, making more fire would only be *worse*.

"Lucy, you're not in trouble, it's okay!"

She was perched on the curtain rod now, keening and rocking in place, and the top of the curtain was starting to lick with flame. The dryer gave a last rattle and then its shrill alert.

Ian got the fire in the bottom of the fabric out and stretched to reach a hand out to her. Where was the nearest stepladder? "Lucy, sweetheart, it's going to be alright. We just have to put the fire out before it hurts the house. Jump to my hand, honey. Come here, right now!" He alternated between begging and scolding. "I have to get the fire extinguisher and put the fire out before it gets bad, but I can't just leave you here." Or hit her with the spray from the extinguisher!

Lucy moved sideways on the curtain rod away from him as the top of the curtain began to burn in earnest.

"Hot!" Ian warned her. "Hot fire! We have to put it out!"

Maybe he did need to wake his dragon. He'd wreck his house shifting, but he'd be able to reach Lucy, and snatch her out of danger, and if his house was going to burn down anyway…

Lucy was looking back and forth between him and the fire in clear alarm, her nose twitching and her whiskers trembling. Then she drew in her breath, like she was going to give a squirrel alarm, and the fire went out.

Ian hadn't realized exactly how noisy the fire was until the crackle went suddenly silent.

The dryer was done.

Lucy was frozen.

The fire was dead. The wall and ceiling were scorched and the paint was bubbled up, but there were only a few weak tendrils of smoke now.

Ian's heart hammering in his ears was the loudest sound in the room and he drew a careful breath. "Hey, Lucy," he said, as gently as he could manage.

She gave a little squeak and leapt for his shoulder, shifting to a little girl when she got there and then sliding down into his arms to weep.

Ian cradled her close and dropped into a seated position on the floor, rocking her as the adrenaline ebbed away.

Just as his heart rate started to slow, the smoke got to the detector in the kitchen and it began to shriek.

Lucy cried and clung to him harder as he stood and Ian kept most of his swearing under his breath as he clambered over Lucy's scooter and the kitchen chairs to get to the screaming alarm and turn it off.

The resulting silence made him feel like he was momentarily deaf and he sank down into one of the chairs as Lucy gradually calmed.

He fished his phone out of a pocket and texted Cherry. *We're staying home tomorrow. Lucy feels a little hot.*

Then he put his phone down on the table and laughed hysterically, until Lucy reached sleepily up and patted his cheek. "Ah good," she said reassuringly. "Ah good."

But was it?

orking at Tiny Paws was sometimes like trying to wade through a field of grasping hands. Every time that she turned around, someone was clinging to Olivia's ankle or begging to be lifted up or tugging on her clothing with a question.

But on her last day of work, it was worse than ever. Amy frankly wailed every time that Olivia put her down, so she ended up carrying her around most of the day.

Even Tara, who was shy with almost everyone, came to her after quiet time and climbed into her lap to give her a tearful hug. "I don't want you to go."

"I'm not going far away," Olivia said. One of the things she was going to miss most about Tiny Paws were the hugs. Middle school students had their own joys, but they were largely not into embracing and cuddling with their teachers. "I'll see you at Lucy's birthday party next month."

Gil spent most of the day as a sullen armadillo, leaving his clothing in piles wherever he'd shifted when he caught sight of Olivia. Jennifer was dramatically sad, sighing and saying tragic things like, "I don't wanna draw. The colors are too sad."

The whole mood of the day care was morose and mopey. Even the babies were whimpery.

Most disappointing of all, Ian canceled bringing Lucy in with a text to Cherry about her feeling hot, so Olivia didn't have the fun of prolonging the morning handoff and flirting with Ian.

"We're going to miss you," Cherry told her frankly during a brief lull late in the early afternoon when the children were mostly pursuing independent play. "Are you sure you haven't changed your mind?"

"I have a one year contract with the school district," Olivia said regretfully, "or I'd be sorely tempted." She was surprised at the truth in the statement that she'd only originally meant as polite.

Olivia herself was not a lot happier than the kids were. She was looking forward to not changing diapers and wiping runny noses, but there was so much she was going to miss, like the comic misspoken words and the darling lisps and the clumsy dancing. She loved watching them learn so much about their own bodies and the world around them, even the babies discovering toes.

She was so happy working here. She enjoyed the trust she'd earned, the way the kids said her name a dozen different ways. And she loved the kids themselves, in all their furry, scaled, or feathered forms.

She was particularly going to miss feeling like a part of something magical here, something she'd always wanted to know was true, reading fairy tales as a child. Something she wanted to be a part of.

If she wasn't working at Tiny Paws, she wouldn't be a part of this amazing secret community that she'd come to love so desperately; going back to work in a mundane school was going to be so *colorless* compared to this.

"Well, keep us in mind if you know anyone who needs a job," Cherry said leadingly. "We could really use another set of hands."

"I see how it is," Olivia teased. "Any warm body!"

They laughed together and Cherry gave her an impulsive hug that Olivia happily returned.

Cherry had been a great boss, cheerful and optimistic, and she never assumed that the job was the most important part of any of her workers' lives. The labor was hard, and she kept a keen eye on all of the people in her charge, making sure that no one was getting burnt out or worn down. She wasn't afraid to step in for the dirtiest and most uncomfortable parts of the job herself, gladly taking a fussy baby or a gross clean-up job to give one of the others a much-needed break. She personally ran at least one of the story times herself every day and the kids loved her as unabashedly as she loved them back.

Olivia thought they might have been good friends under other circumstances, and she would have loved to sit with Cherry and ask her about running a shifter day care when she wasn't a shifter herself, even after nearly a month of knowing about shifters and magic, she had a lot of questions she wasn't sure how to ask.

But Cherry was already running full speed by the time Olivia got in, and long after she left. As far as Olivia could tell, she was there every open hour, as well as every late pickup and every early morning drop off.

The few times that Olivia tried to ask Cherry about herself, either they were interrupted by a needy child, or Cherry neatly worked the conversation back around to Olivia instead, so deftly that Olivia wasn't really sure how they got there.

"Thank you so much for the opportunity," Olivia said warmly. "This is one of the best jobs I've ever had."

"You've been a joy," Cherry said sincerely. "Come back and be a warm body any time."

Gabby and Amy were having a noisy conflict over a prized toy and Addison was busy with the babies so Cherry went to mediate.

For a job that paid as much in wilted flowers and snotty hugs as it did in money, it really was the best job of her life.

CHAPTER 19

When the front doorbell rang the next morning, Ian had a moment of glee and anticipation, then a moment of confusion. Why wouldn't Olivia be at the *back* door?

Then he remembered Wanda.

Wanda was taking Lucy to see her folks over Labor Day weekend. He'd noticed it on the calendar a few times, but it hadn't occurred to him until that very moment the rest of what that meant: that he had a weekend without her.

Ian glanced at the time. Wanda was always ferociously punctual, and here she was, ten minutes early. Ian suspected that she usually came a few minutes ahead hoping to watch him rush around in a panic trying to get Lucy ready to go. He was in the habit of having her ready fifteen minutes early and had a moment of annoyance that he hadn't remembered to do that this time.

Lucy was still eating breakfast, having a conversation with her scrambled eggs that seemed to relate to Seltzer and Gabby. Her fork was more of a percussion instrument than an eating utensil. She looked up in surprise at the doorbell.

"Your mom is here!" Ian said, as brightly as he could manage.

Lucy abandoned her eggs to climb down. Ian caught her with a washcloth for her hands before she could touch more than her chair, tossing it back for a perfect shot into the sink. No one ever saw *those* shots.

"Mummy!" Lucy cried, pelting for the front door. "Mummy!"

Ian never wanted to make Lucy a pawn between himself and Wanda, so he always hid how it hurt when his daughter seemed to prefer her mother, despite the fact that he was her primary parent these days. He would never let Lucy know that he had anything but respect for Wanda, making sure not to speak poorly about her in front of her or argue with her when Lucy was around.

Wanda didn't return that courtesy, and Ian was sure it made him look like a doormat.

At least his dragon was slumbering, so he didn't have anyone *else* reminding him that he looked spineless and offering a lot of advice about what he should do and say.

"Is she ready to go?" Wanda asked curtly when he opened the door. She patted Lucy absently on the head as Lucy threw arms around her knees. "Hi, darling. I want to get out before the traffic gets bad."

"It's nice to see you too," Ian said, not entirely able to keep the bite from his voice. He was able to grab her bag from the hook by the door and hand it to Wanda without fuss. "There are some snacks in there, and night-time diapers."

It was all leftover from day care the day before, but Wanda didn't have to know that.

She took it and looked through it skeptically. "Well, I'm

sure you're looking forward to having the weekend all by yourself," she said. "You'll have plenty of time to work on your next big bestseller."

Was it a dig on the fact that Wanda thought he wasn't capable of dating, as well as a thinly veiled insult to his stuttering career? Ian glanced down at the top of Lucy's head. "Sezzer wobble digger," she said.

Ian couldn't puzzle a logical sentence out of her words and didn't try for long. "Oh," he remembered. "She'll need her stuffy from her bed."

"Sezzer!" Lucy cried, and she peeled herself from Wanda's knees to flee back to her room.

"She renamed her stuffed flamingo Seltzer after the cat next door," Ian explained.

Wanda's eyes snapped in alarm. "There's a cat next door? Is it an outdoor cat?"

"They're great friends," Ian assured her. He would just skip the part where the cat had caught Lucy and nearly given Ian a heart attack. "They play together all the time."

Wanda pounced. "You're letting her play with a *cat*?"

"Only supervised," Ian protested. Everything he did seemed stupid when Wanda said it. He recognized that this was a brief chance to talk to Wanda without Lucy listening and remembered what else he needed to tell her. "They're fine together. Look, there's something you need to know. Lucy's been an extra handful recently…"

As he was figuring out how to explain *by the way, our daughter now breathes fire*, Wanda sniffed.

"I know that it's *hard* chasing an energetic squirrel child. I don't blame you for putting her in day care."

The way she said it put Ian's back up, like she was speaking from a place of superiority and pretending to be sympathetic.

"It's not just that she's a squirrel, Wanda," Ian said

through gritted teeth. "Or that she's active, it's that now she can—"

Wanda plowed right over him. "You grew up an only child, and you never had younger siblings to take care of. I'm sure that day care seemed like *your* only option."

Everything about her tone said *you can't hack it.*

Ian was glad that his dragon was asleep.

If it had been awake, the least the dragon would have done was steam unhelpfully in his ear, and Ian felt hot enough already; he could almost smell the sulfur on his breath. He'd been Lucy's primary carer for more than a year now, and he'd all but given up his career for her. He was the one who lost sleep when she was teething, he was the one who was scraping to make the day care payments.

His dragon would have been on his other shoulder, grumbling about the fact that Ian wasn't standing up for himself, as if Ian wasn't already battling for control of his powers.

Ian couldn't trust himself to speak for a moment.

"There's something you should know," he said, as calmly as he could, when his mouth would work again.

"I'm sure you find it very challenging," Wanda scoffed impatiently. "Lucy, are you ready to go? We're in a hurry, honey!"

Ian thought he should warn her. He should take the high ground and fight to tell her the information she clearly wasn't interested in hearing.

But he was also furious, tired of being weak with her, and just petty enough to make her find out the same way that he had.

He swallowed, tasting smoke, then knelt to give Lucy and stuffed-Seltzer a hug. "I'm going to miss you, sweetie," he said honestly. "I love you."

"Wuv oo."

He was keenly aware of Wanda's critical eye as he brushed scrambled egg from Lucy's dress. "Be good for your mom, okay?" He leaned close and whispered, "*No fires.*" Lucy hadn't set any fires at all since the incident, and the only smoke he smelled now was his own. Maybe it was a fluke. Maybe it wouldn't be a problem at all.

Lucy nodded solemnly, one hand creeping into her mouth like it did when she was stressed or serious about something. Ian gave her another big hug and kissed her forehead. "I'll see you on Monday."

As she scampered down the sidewalk with her hand in Wanda's, Ian told himself again that she was unlikely to light anything on fire again. She'd been completely chagrined about the accident and showed no signs of doing it again. Probably, it wouldn't come up at all that weekend. It wasn't really like he was sabotaging Wanda.

Not exactly.

He breathed out, not sure if the smoke he smelled was psychosomatic or not, then took in the sudden quiet of the house. He was childfree for the entire weekend. Just a few weeks earlier, he'd have opened his laptop to take advantage of his unexpected writing time. But he was making solid progress on his book, and there was another thing he could do without Lucy underfoot, something he'd been dying to do.

Something that it was long past time he did.

He looked around the little house. It was a wreck even before the curtains had caught on fire and singed the wall and carpet, and a weekend of intense cleaning and home repair was not at all what he had in mind.

He dialed his phone.

"Belle Lake Lodge," Curtis Nanuk answered, sounding totally business. "How can I assist you?"

"Wow, man, you've gotten boring," Ian scoffed. "It's Ian."

"Ian? Long time no talk! What are you doing these days? I got your book at Under the Covers, isn't there supposed to be a sequel by now?"

Ian was surprised and flattered that Curtis had followed his career—such as it was—since high school. "I'm working on it," he said. "Do I need a reservation for the restaurant out there at the lodge?"

"Nah," Curtis said. "We don't get a lot of random traffic and we're only about half full right now. It's been hard to get bookings with the short term leases charging so much less. You remember Veronica Chase?"

"I remember," Ian said wryly. "She tried to buy the house I'm leasing out from under me. Is she still making trouble in the rentals market?"

"She can rent a whole house for the price that we have to charge for a single room. Who's going to drive an hour out of town for the privilege of a more expensive stay? I mean, the view is great, but it's not *that* great."

Ian thought about Olivia's face when she'd suggested a date for that weekend. He wasn't that great with women, but she seemed…interested. Flirty, even. When his dragon was awake, it was sure that she was everything, that she was the one and only, and that her interest in him was as keen as his fascination with her.

"Do you have any rooms left this weekend? Maybe at a really steep old friend's discount?"

"Oh, looking for a weekend out with the old lady? I heard you got married."

Ian winced. "Yeah. Divorced."

"Oh, sorry."

"It was more than a year ago," Ian said, and he wondered why it felt like an entire lifetime and only a few days, all at the same time. "I've got a new girl—" Girlfriend seemed presumptive. Then again, booking a room at a resort was pretty presumptive, too. "I'm seeing someone. Seriously, maybe."

"Yeah, sounds like, if you're looking for a hot Labor Day retreat. I think I have a famous writer's suite available."

"I don't know for sure," Ian said firmly. "We're just going to start with dinner and then play it by ear."

"Like I said, it's been hard to fill rooms. I'll pencil you in. It'll be good to see you again!"

Ian hung up with something suspiciously like hope in his chest and then stared at his phone.

After a moment, he heaved a great sigh and texted Wanda: *Our daughter can breathe fire now.*

Wanda replied with a laughing emoji.

Well, he'd tried.

Now he just had to figure out how to ask Olivia.

CHAPTER 20

Olivia thought it was a little ridiculous to get excited over Ian's contact information on her phone when it rang. He was, after all, her next-door neighbor. He was probably calling to see if Seltzer had caught Lucy again, or to borrow a cup of sugar.

Olivia wished that he would borrow *her* cup of sugar.

But even though she thought it was pretty obvious that they were really into each other, it never seemed to be the right time. Either she was at the day care being run ragged by tiny shifters with sticky hands or she was at home trying to recover from their tender abuse, or he was chasing Lucy, or Lucy was hollering for help from the bathroom. They had brief conversations at the driveway when they happened to be out at the same time, and they waved shyly through their windows that looked into each other's houses, but every time, without fail, that Olivia thought he was going to ask her out again, they were interrupted or he shut down on her.

So, she was surprised when he opened the conversation

with a bold, "I know it's really short warning, but do you want to go out of town with me for dinner?"

Olivia's heart gave a happy little flip-flop. "Tonight? Out of town?"

"Wanda's got Lucy for the weekend and I thought I could take you out," Ian said in a rush. "One of those… surprise dates that I don't tell you where we're going and we go on a magnificent scenic tour and I sweep you off your feet."

"You're not going to tell me where you're taking me?" Olivia said. He was so nervous that it was adorable, and she didn't feel an awful lot more calm. It had been a long time since she'd had a crush like this and she worried that she was letting her heart run away with her head.

"No, it's a secret," Ian said. "But…oh wait, you might need some things. Girl things or whatever. Okay, fine, I'm taking you to Belle Lake Lodge. I know the owner. And they have really good food. And if you wanted to stay overnight, I've reserved a room. For two nights. But I wasn't going to tell you that part unless the dinner went really well. Oh my god, I'm so bad at this."

Olivia had walked into the kitchen, which was the window that looked over into his house and caught sight of him in his own kitchen, the phone at his ear, so she could witness his facepalm. They waved at each other and Olivia had to laugh. "I think that sounds great," she said, wondering if her blush would show through two sets of windows. Probably not. She could barely make Ian's smile out through the glare. "I mean, not the room, *necessarily*. We could…ah…play that by ear?"

"That would be fine. Absolutely fine. Great. Amazing." Ian flashed her a thumbs up and a grin so wide that his eyes all but disappeared.

"I have to set up my classroom this afternoon," Olivia

said slowly, twisting a lock of her hair. "How far away is the lodge?"

"It's about an hour's drive," Ian said. "It's not that far as the crow flies, but the road's really windy."

As the crow flies. Olivia wondered suddenly if Ian was something that could fly. Her breath caught at the whole idea of it. She really wanted to ask what he was. It was eating at her that she didn't know. But she didn't want to be rude, and the topic seemed to make him nervous.

Seltzer was twining around her ankles making conversational noises, like a child that wanted to use her phone. Olivia stooped to pet him and this brought her to eye-level with one of her framed photographs, still sitting out on a box because she hadn't bought hanging hardware yet. "Hey, I…" she hesitated.

"What is it?"

"Would you mind if I brought my camera and we stopped to take a few pictures?"

"Why would I mind?"

"I don't know, maybe you're one of those guys who wants to go from point A to point B without a bunch of stops to take photographs of flowers and dead grass?"

Ian chuckled. "I don't know if you noticed or not, but I have a little girl who takes me from point A to point Q, and backwards through the alphabet in random order. Getting directly from point A to point B is not a thing that single dads get to do. We can stop as many times as you want. I promise I'm used to it."

Olivia felt her face crinkle in amusement. "Yeah, I've noticed that about Lucy. The trip to the trashcan after snack is an entire expedition with an enthusiastic guide! Shall I meet you in the driveway at five?"

"That sounds great. Amazing. Fantastic."

"I'll see you then."

"Yeah. At five. In the driveway. Wait, whose driveway?"

It was an absurd question, because the driveways were side-by-side, separated only by the low front fence, so Olivia giggled. "How about your driveway? I'll wear comfortable shoes and walk all the way over."

"I could drive over and honk from the road," Ian teased.

"So classy!" Olivia laughed.

"In the driveway. My driveway. At five."

"Driveway," she repeated. "Your driveway. At five."

When she finally hung up, feeling like a reluctant teenager, Olivia's phone was nearly out of battery; it was getting old and less reliable, but new phones were expensive. She smiled foolishly at it and then plugged it in.

A weekend retreat to a Montana mountain lodge with the hot next-door neighbor and not a kid in sight for two whole nights? It was silly, spontaneous, and sort of…perfect.

It was also about damn time.

Olivia bent down and picked Seltzer up to twirl around a few cuddly steps. He squirmed in protest, but couldn't quite keep from purring, his big paws kneading claws straight through her shirt. "Ow, ow!" Olivia said. "Tough love."

She put him back down on the floor and he immediately began to groom off Olivia's presumptive touch.

Olivia could not get the invitation out of her mind. She walked to the middle school and went through the routine of setting up her classroom. It didn't take much work; middle school students didn't really go in for a lot of cutesy room decoration. She hung up her periodic table and Einstein inspirational poster and she'd confirmed that the gas and water hookups were in working order. She made sure she could log into her admin account, and the name on the door was spelled right.

Her name! At the door of *her* classroom!

Then she locked the room and went back home to throw together a weekend overnight bag.

Seltzer would be fine for two nights alone and Olivia filled his water dish to the brim and dumped extra dry food in his bowl, knowing that he would stuff himself into a stupor the first day and then spend the second day complaining because he could see the bottom of the dish and there was no one around to fill it back up or give him the worship he was due.

She packed her bag, throwing in a swimsuit and a few changes of clothing. She charged her camera battery and checked the cards. The familiar habits were bittersweet after so long, and Olivia felt like maybe she'd finally laid all of her pain and resentment to rest.

This was a new town, with new friends and opportunities.

And maybe even new love.

CHAPTER 21

*J*an turned onto the rough gravel road and shut the radio off. It was pointless to have it on while they were traveling the rough road to Belle Lake Lodge.

"This is a road?" Olivia exclaimed. "It's not even paved."

"Once you get off the main highways, most of them aren't. There are a lot of them that shouldn't be driven after heavy rains. There's nothing left but mud."

"How can there be so much *nothing* in Montana?" Olivia asked as they followed the winding road through forest and canyon. "We haven't seen a car in a half an hour!"

It was dry, and a plume of dust followed them on the road.

The hour-long drive out to Belle Lake Lodge ended up taking closer to two and a half hours. Every time there was a wide spot in the road, Ian pulled over before she could ask and Olivia hopped out to photograph something—the sun through trees, the sky red with the smoke from the nearby wildfires, or a tiny flower in a stand of dead grass. She seemed particularly fascinated with unusual rock faces.

Some of her choices baffled Ian, who only saw more dry underbrush and the same dull trees and rocks as ever. But Olivia's enthusiasm was contagious, and when he caught her snapping sly photographs of him, he challenged her to pose for him in return.

"It's only fair!" he told her, laughing and holding out his hand.

"Here," she said, handing him the camera and standing tantalizingly close to slip the strap over his head. "It's in full automatic mode, you shouldn't have to adjust anything. Just point the lens, then there's the shutter button. Press it down a little and it will autofocus, then click it to take a photo. It's digital, so take as many as you like, no film to waste."

"Oh my gosh, I remember photos when I was a little kid," Ian said. "Expensive to develop, always running out of film, had to wait a week to find out half the roll was shots of the ground."

Ian took some photos that even he could tell were pedestrian, Olivia looking awkward and uncomfortable as she posed in front of a green sign proclaiming 30 miles to Belle Lake Lodge. Not a single car passed them by as he took shot after shot. "You have to smile!" he scolded her. "You look like I'm torturing you!"

"I *am* smiling!" she protested, looking more wooden than ever. "I hate this side of a camera!"

Ian lowered the camera. "Why would you?" he asked in astonishment. "You're the most beautiful person I've ever met in my life."

The effect on Olivia was astonishing. Her big, forced smile softened into wonder and surprise. "I…you… that's…"

Ian remembered to snap a photograph of her, not sure if it was in focus or even if she was actually in the frame.

Yes, his dragon purred. *She is a work of art. She is perfect.*

Human aesthetics weren't a thing that Ian had ever thought his dragon cared for in the slightest. Indeed, his dragon had been something of a surprise on this entire trip, not once criticizing Ian or calling his confidence into question. It was *there*, alert and watching, and Ian had that unsettling sense of instinct like a conversation just out of earshot, but he didn't feel like he was a specimen in some greater species' petri dish, being judged for every word and action or yanked along like a poorly behaved dog on a leash.

His dragon felt like a partner, at least for the moment, like they were aligned in their feeling that this, here with Olivia, was where they belonged. It wasn't just that Ian was looking forward to hopefully taking her to one of the lodge rooms and stripping her naked to claim her—though there was certainly some of that going on inside him, too.

It was more that he *liked* being part of this playful, creative side of her, watching her find beauty in the scenery he'd always taken for granted, being included in her excitement. For once, he and Olivia weren't running after a toddler or bouncing off to their next commitment. It was delicious to have the time for leisure, to stop and play.

It made Ian think wistfully of growing old with this woman and retiring to a life of quiet pleasures.

Yes, his dragon purred. *Our Olivia!*

"I've probably made us late for our dinner," Olivia said, taking the camera back shyly, her real smile still dancing on her lips and in her eyes.

"I know the owner," Ian said. "He'll make sure we don't go hungry, no matter how late we get there." Olivia put her camera back in the case without looking back through the photos he'd taken and Ian politely held the door for her.

As he got into the driver's seat, Ian realized that he'd never told her any of how he felt.

He figured it was obvious how head-over-heels he was with her, but he'd never *told* her she was pretty or explained how crazy and *alive* she made him feel.

It was hard being romantic while under the scrutiny of a nosy toddler.

He should have taken up Rod's offer for a second date, but it felt like too much of an imposition. He knew first-hand how much trouble Lucy could be. He winced. Especially now that she was breathing fire.

He hadn't thought about Lucy's alarming new gift once since they left, but he wondered if she'd done it again, and how Wanda was dealing with it, if she had. He checked his phone, but they were in a cell shadow and he had no signal. The lodge would have spotty wi-fi, but the night (and maybe the weekend!) would not have cell phone connection. Ian put his phone in airplane mode so it wouldn't wear out the battery searching for a signal. As long as his dragon was alert, instinct would warn him if Lucy needed him, and it would have suggested it to him now if leaving her with Wanda had been the wrong move, he comforted himself. The dragon was quiet and content, for the moment.

Eventually, the terrible road took them circuitously around to overlook the northern shore of the sprawling Belle Lake.

Olivia was so awed by the view that for several moments after they got out of the car, she forgot to take photographs. "It's beautiful," she breathed.

She wasn't wrong. The sunset was more spectacular

than usual, stained particularly vivid hues of red by the wildfire smoke that hung in the air, and it reflected on the surface of Belle Lake like a pane of fiery glass. They were high here, but the mountains around them were higher yet, craggy and caught with threads of rust and gold. A few clouds smudged the sky in hot magenta and the backlit edges of the peaks across the lake were so bright that it looked like they were traced in molten metal.

Olivia remembered the camera around her neck and snapped a few photos out over the railing. "I thought we'd be down by the lake," she said. "I was expecting a…beach and a dock. Maybe a moose."

"There is a dock," Ian told her. "I don't know about a moose." Should he get their luggage? They were still playing it by ear, so it would probably be presumptuous. "They have some canoes. It's a two-mile hike almost straight downhill, which isn't too bad, but coming back up is a serious workout. Roderick and Curtis and I used to race it."

"Ooo," Olivia said. She looked down the bluff. "Maybe tomorrow."

Hope leapt up in Ian's throat. That meant…?

"*If* we decide to stay," she added with one quick sideways glance.

The hope burst like an overblown bubble.

That doesn't mean she will say no, his dragon reminded him crossly. *Don't borrow doom from a future we don't know.*

I wasn't borrowing doom, Ian protested.

Ian had liked his dragon's quiet companionship on their trip and sourly wished that he'd go back to it.

CHAPTER 22

*D*inner was delicious, but Olivia felt like the entire meal was a complicated act of culinary foreplay.

They were both keenly aware of the room waiting for them upstairs. Playing it by ear meant *maybe*, but Olivia's whole body was tuned to *yes*.

She wanted to be bold and forward. No guy had ever set her on fire quite like this.

They talked lightly about Ian's book, about Olivia's classes, dancing around the topic of shifters with wary glances at the other guests at the restaurant.

They talked about Lucy, and laughed over stories of her antics.

"Seltzer's crazy for her," Olivia told him frankly. "I've never seen him so attached to anyone before."

"He's a pretty amazing cat," Ian said. "He's like…a dog."

"Don't let him hear you say that," Olivia chuckled. "He is quite convinced of his species' superiority."

She wasn't quite sure why Ian laughed so hard about

that, but everything about the dinner had been easy humor and conversation like they had been friends forever. They had so much common ground to work from that it was occasionally eerie, and they quoted the same books and television shows at each other almost effortlessly. When they did find a disconnect of media, they each assured the other that they had to read or watch it or listen to it with easy confidence that "...you will *love* it."

It was like she'd known him for years and they were reconnecting after a long absence. Or maybe a short absence. Maybe a short, hot, long-distance relationship, separated only by a fence.

When they had savored the steaks and licked the last of the brownie sundaes up, there was a moment of pause.

"Anything else for you folks?"

Olivia was pretty sure that the hulking guy who was waiting their table was the owner of the lodge. Ian had introduced him as Curtis, and the two of them had exchanged a big bear hug when they arrived.

"Nothing for me," she assured him. "It was all amazing."

"I couldn't pack in another bite if I wanted to," Ian added. "Not one wafer-thin Yum-Yum. Tell Archer he should be cooking at one of those New York restaurants."

Curtis looked pleased. "I'm not going to tell him that. He'll move there and leave us to serve boxed macaroni and cheese and oven-baked chicken tenders because that's all the rest of us can cook."

"I would be right at home with that," Ian confessed with a chuckle. "I should get stock in those oven chicken tenders, it's sometimes all that Lucy will eat."

Curtis smirked. "I'll put this on your *room bill*," he said pointedly, and then he sailed away to refill someone else's water.

Olivia toyed with her napkin. There was a room bill because there was a *room*. A room where the two of them could go *right now*.

Ian didn't assume anything, though, and he offered quietly, "I haven't had too much to drink to drive you back to Nickel City."

He hadn't either. Olivia was sure that it wasn't just a careless over-estimation of his own ability to hold it (though it did occur to Olivia to wonder if being a whatever-shifter gave him a higher tolerance to alcohol); he had accepted only a single beer at the beginning of the meal. Olivia had matched him, keeping to one glass of wine. She'd wondered wistfully if she'd be braver with more, but whatever happened between her and Ian, she wanted to meet it with a clear mind.

But even if it wasn't fuzzed with alcohol, her mind was far from clear.

She wanted this guy in carnal ways that complicated all her common sense. She should keep things practical, and having a fiery wild hotel fling with her hot next-door neighbor might make their relationship awkward if that's all it turned out to be. Part of her said that she should be cautious and take it slow. Part of her howled that she'd waited nearly a month already and if they went any slower she was going to grow moss on her lady bits.

Olivia licked her lips, tasting salt and chocolate and wine she didn't feel.

Ian was watching her, waiting for her answer, and she searched his face for it. It was obvious that he wanted her as badly as she wanted him. Everyone in the restaurant could probably tell from the way they were laughing together and gazing at each other and telling each other silly life stories for the first time.

It had been a perfect date. She was either going to ruin

it now and disappoint them both, or she was going to take the risk that they might be amazing together.

"What room did you say we had?" she asked quietly

Ian forgot about the napkin in his lap as he stood, and had to stoop to pick it up. That gave Olivia a chance to scramble to her own feet and then he took her hand. "Our luggage is still in the car," she reminded him, and although they started sedately, they were pelting like sugared-up preschoolers when they hit the parking lot.

~

"*O*h no," Olivia said drolly as she unlocked the door and opened it into the gorgeous lodge suite. "There's only one bed!"

It was a charming room, with a sitting area and a huge bed covered in a quaint patchwork quilt. The walls and floor were gleaming wood, and there were French doors out onto a porch that looked out over the lake. The decor was all cabin-rustic, with flying ducks and mountain land-scapes and lots of plaid. It smelled slightly of smoke, which might have been from the nearby wildfires, or from the little fireplace across from the couch where a pile of kindling waited to be lit. There was no television.

"What are we going to do?" Ian asked in mock horror. "How will we ever contain our animal passions?"

Olivia reminded herself that he actually *had* animal passions. Some kind of animal, anyway. "Maybe we don't," she suggested slyly.

To her delight, Ian dropped their luggage (he had insisted on carrying her bag along with his) and kicked the door shut behind him. His arms were exactly where she belonged, and his kiss was exactly what her mouth had wanted, that whole delicious meal. She threw her purse onto a chair by the door and wrapped her arms around him.

For the moment, she didn't care about his secrets or his single-dad complications. She only cared that she was absolutely on fire for him, and ready to let down all of her walls.

Olivia had feared that she'd built up her memory of their kiss into something that it wasn't, that trying again would have been chasing a fantasy. But this kiss was *even hotter*. Was it because she knew what would happen next? Was it because she'd gotten to know even more about him since then? She didn't really care *why*, she was alive now, in this moment, and she wanted him closer and deeper, more and more with every desperate kiss.

"Olivia," he said, drawing away for the moment.

They had gotten halfway into the room, though Olivia didn't actually remember taking any steps.

"Ian?" she teased him. She was ready to be wearing a whole lot less.

"Olivia, I think I love you."

Olivia had never had such a physical reaction to spoken words before. She went from panting desire to a spike of unexpected passion just shy of an actual orgasm. "You...*me?*" she said incoherently. She couldn't quite say the word *love* herself.

His hands were on either side of her face, fingers twined up into her loose hair. "I love you," he said again, more firmly.

Olivia wondered if she should say it back, with a sudden stab of worry because—what if she didn't love him? She didn't have a magical instinct to tell her which path was best. She knew he was still keeping secrets from her. She'd never been any good at *love*.

Fortunately, he didn't seem to expect actual words out

of her, and when he kissed her, Olivia forgot how to speak
altogether.

CHAPTER 23

*I*an was afraid he'd screwed up, telling Olivia that he loved her. He should have waited, so it didn't seem like it was just about the sex they were on the brink of. He should have made *sure* that she was as serious as he was. He shouldn't have put her on the spot so completely.

But instead of ruining the moment, it only seemed to heighten their intensity, and when she kissed him again, Ian thought that Olivia felt even brighter in his mouth, even more pliable against his whole body.

His dragon was avid, but quiet in his head, and the out-of-sync feedback-prickle that Ian usually felt with his presence was muted. Ian unbuttoned Olivia's shirt, tiny, complicated button after button, not rushing, though his fingers trembled a little in anticipation. She was still while he slipped her blouse from her shoulders, then returned the favor in a ritual that Ian knew he was never going to be able to perform without thinking of her again.

She was wearing a tapestry-patterned maroon bra with little bows at the straps, somehow both proper and flirty.

Ian couldn't decide if he wanted it off of her more than he wanted it on her, cupping overflowing breasts absolutely perfectly.

He slipped a finger under one strap and drew it off her shoulder so that it fell away from the top, not quite uncovering a nipple. He dragged a thumb over her exposed skin and she gave a hiss of pleasure, then took her hands back to unclasp the bra and let it drop away altogether.

Bare breasts were better, he decided immediately, and he didn't give conscious commands to his hands before they were caressing the mesmerizing curves.

Time didn't really have much meaning anymore; Ian wasn't sure if he was standing there, reverently touching the lines of her body, for a few minutes or an hour. He only knew that her soft, sweet skin was more intoxicating than anything he'd ever felt in his entire life, and the silky fall of her hair was like music.

She shimmied out of her pants and Ian had just enough brain receptors still firing to figure out how to get out of his own jeans, hampered by the size and stiffness of his hard-on.

"Olivia," he groaned, reaching for her again. His hands missed her even in that short time.

And there was no clothing now, keeping them apart.

"Ian," she breathed, when they touched again, her hand on his cock, his at her waist.

"Condom," he remembered. "I brought condoms."

He'd thrown an entire unopened box into his suitcase, but now he wished he'd put one into his pocket, because he was clumsy with eagerness and unzipping his luggage was challenging enough even before he got to the sealed container.

"Why would they make these boxes so hard to get

into?" he asked in giddy frustration, trying to tear off the plastic and keep his balance.

Hurry, his dragon urged.

Olivia was no help, giggling and kissing and teasing him and touching herself. Ian actually dropped the box watching her trail a finger down her belly to caress lightly between her legs.

"How are you so hot?" he asked.

The question seemed to delight her.

The box finally opened and he ripped a sealed condom off the strip. The individual package opened easily, at least, and then he was sheathing himself in thin plastic and tackling Olivia to sheath himself in *her*.

It was desperate and fast, even though Ian thought they were both trying to prolong things. He took her fiercely, tangled together on top of the bed. It had an unexpected amount of bounce, but it took only a moment to figure out a resonant rhythm, and Olivia cried out in release just moments before he lost his own resolve and fell from a cliff of pleasure.

Even though it was short and urgent, Ian felt like it was absolutely perfect, and Olivia was laughing happily and gasping for breath.

"How are *you* so hot?" she wanted to know, as they lay together after cleaning up.

Ian didn't want to stop touching her, even though the edge of their need had been dulled, and they cuddled on top of the quilt.

"You set me on fire," he said. It was starting to get chilly, and when she shivered, he reluctantly let go of her to start the fire that was laid out in the fireplace.

When he returned to the bed, she'd put on a shirt, to his disappointment. But no underwear, to his delight. Was it an unspoken invitation for more? He felt surprising stirrings that suggested it wouldn't be long before he would be up for a second round.

His dragon seemed to purr in his head, not being pushy or impatient.

It was still plenty of fun to snuggle with Olivia through her thin shirt, and they kissed and talked and kissed and talked and Ian wasn't even sure when they started making love again. It was much simpler to get the second condom out of the box, and it was Olivia that slid it onto him.

Time stopped having meaning again as he pulled off her shirt, lay her down and thrust into her. She was so responsive and eager and they fit together so perfectly. They were tempered, this time, exploring methods and positions one after another.

He bent her down over a pile of pillows and found an angle to enter her from behind that made her lose all control and cry out, slowing to prolong her orgasm deliciously. They lay spooned together and he slipped into her, holding the whole length of her gorgeous, curved body against his. He held her down by the wrists and dragged his teeth along her neck while he thrust into her harder and harder.

And finally, he lay and let her straddle him, the beautiful, lush figure of her in sweet motion as she rode him. He held her waist and hips and lost the last of his control to come hard, making a helpless, guttural noise of completion.

He was lost for some time after that, Olivia collapsed on his chest, her hair like cool water over his bare skin, buried deep inside of her as long as flesh allowed it.

They showered together, smiling foolishly and touching each other shyly, and Ian felt as if he'd accomplished some herculean task, or leveled up in some fashion. It wasn't just the hum of satisfaction, and it wasn't the still-swirling hint of instinct that was trying to prod him in some unknown direction.

This was where he belonged, forever and always.

Not necessarily in this room, at this lodge, but with this woman, complete at last.

Even his dragon was happy.

CHAPTER 24

Olivia woke in darkness, confused for a moment because the weight behind her wasn't Seltzer. It was Ian, she recognized quickly, and he was breathing evenly in her hair. There was a hard-on pressing against her, and one of his arms was tucked around her.

The room was dark and cool and the fire had gone out, but Olivia could see a twinkle of the lodge porch lights through the windows; they hadn't pulled the drapes.

She was blissfully content, her whole body feeling satisfied. She was safe and comfortable. Ian was warm against her, and the sheets felt amazing against her bare skin. It would have been easy to go back to sleep and the idea surprised her. She'd always felt uncomfortable when she slept over with someone, or had them over to her place, like they didn't belong in her bed. She wanted her own space, her own blankets.

But this felt so right.

Is that what instinct was like? she wondered wistfully.

She pressed back against Ian, loving the feel of his cock

against her, and he murmured and held her closer, his hand coming awake to squeeze her breast and then caress down her body towards her vulva.

He didn't say anything, but he kissed her neck and grazed his fingers just over her clit. Olivia couldn't quite keep from writhing against him, surprised by how immediately he was able to arouse her again. He dipped one finger slowly into her, and she was already wet and ready.

She reached around him to return the favor, stroking his cock gently and dragging her nails over his balls. He held her tighter, but kept his finger just inside her lips as he nibbled at her neck.

Olivia couldn't have said how long they did that, teasing each other and making tiny noises of pleasure, before he rose up on his knees and rolled her over so that he could straddle her, pressing himself against her.

"Condom," he murmured, freezing in place as if he'd only just then come awake. Maybe he had.

Olivia feared they'd lose the momentum, but he managed to deftly dismount, turn on the jarring light, sheath himself, turn the light back off, and return to the bed with remarkable speed. If anything, the glimpse of his lean, built body turned her on even more, and the darkness when the light turned off was even richer.

He didn't assume that they were coming back to the same place he'd left off and he paused to touch her into readiness again, stroking her clit, caressing her breasts, kissing her neck until she was whimpering and begging for him.

His entrance was slow and sure, and it was completely different not being able to see anything in the darkness. Olivia's world narrowed to his intoxicating touches, the way he filled her, the way they moved together, his noises… and hers.

This love making was slower than their athletic adventures of the night before, more tender, and Olivia found herself reaching the same heights and falling in completely new ways.

She checked the time when they washed up. It was three in the morning. "Do you think there are northern lights?" she asked wistfully. They were supposed to be visible in Montana sometimes but the neighborhood lights of Crescent Drive kept the night sky from being clear.

Ian was game to go out with her onto the balcony and look, but the sky looked smudged. The stars were blurred and faint, and there was a reddish glow over the mountains.

"I think it's too smoky to see them, if they're even there," Ian said.

"Do you think the fires are close?" Wildfire wasn't common in the area of Florida she came from, and the whole idea of them made Olivia uneasy.

"No," Ian said with casual confidence. "Smoke travels a long way. We're safe here."

Olivia shivered and they went back inside and dived under the covers together.

The alarm that Ian set so they wouldn't miss breakfast went off on time, but they missed the meal anyway, making love again and then lingering in the shower together.

Olivia ate a protein bar from the vending machine and sat on the balcony with Ian drinking coffee. Any lingering fears that having sex would change their easy friendliness vanished with their conversation. They talked about Lucy, and about their own childhoods. She had grown up in the south and had seven nosy Latina aunts and three sisters that Olivia was just as happy to have at the arm's length of social media. He was an only child who had homeschooled until high school. His father had died when he was in middle school and he had a degree in English.

"It's natural that I became a writer," he joked. "I'm used to being antisocial and isolated."

She had always known that she wanted to be a teacher. "I taught for three years in Baton Rouge, but I think I read too many Little House books, because I always wanted to come and be a tough teacher in a one-room log classroom, you know? I found the Nickel City opening online and it just sounded…perfect. A place where I could *belong*."

It felt perfect, at this moment. Her whole body tingled with satisfaction, she was drinking delicious coffee looking out over a view that was straight off of a postcard, sitting just opposite from a great, big-hearted guy that she was absolutely crazy about.

"Is it everything you'd hoped?" he asked. He was so handsome, with his golden-brown eyes and his unbuttoned shirt.

"Ask me after the students come back," she laughed.

They didn't spend the whole day having sex, but they did make love again before lunch, Ian's unbuttoned shirt too much to resist.

They explored the lodge itself and Olivia had to drag herself out of the fairy tale library. It had shelves up to big vaulted ceilings filled with books, complete with sliding ladders. A sign picturing a crossed-out Disney princess suggested that she was not allowed to ride them for fun and she and Ian both lamented this tragic overregulation.

"What's the point of a library if you can't joy-ride in it?" Ian wanted to know.

There was a big shared hot tub out on the far side of the deck that they vowed to make use of before they left.

Lunch was burgers, far from basic, with thick, fresh fries and a basil aioli.

"Justin grows his own basil," Curtis explained. "We're trying to find ways to use it up before it takes over the tomatoes."

After lunch, they hiked down to the lake and used one of the lodge canoes to go out on the water.

Ian pointed out places from his misspent youth, and warned her away from the beach in an inviting little bay. "Old Man Caleb lives there and he's not at all friendly. He's a shifter, and Curtis swears that he eats trespassers. There are some hot springs way back on his property—we got chased out of them with a shotgun once."

They paddled around for an hour or so, nearly capsized when she got excited about a fish, and raced back up the steep trail side-by-side.

They arrived at the lodge panting and sweaty. Olivia felt like she'd just run a marathon and could barely suck air into her lungs. Ian, damn him, looked like he'd just gone on an easy evening stroll.

"I wouldn't have been able to do that at all if I hadn't spent the last month chasing kids around at Tiny Paws," she confessed, gulping down a bottled water.

Ian flexed a muscle at her. "Toddler deadlifts," he joked. "Best workout ever."

Apparently, she was still appealing even covered in sweat, and she didn't make it to the shower before Ian was stripping off the rest of her clothes and taking her bent over the couch.

"I think that was an even better workout," she laughed, when they were both spent and lying on the cool floor.

"Five stars," Ian agreed, finally looking disheveled himself. "I highly recommend this fitness plan."

After her delayed shower, Olivia thought they might really be done for the weekend. She was deliciously sore and tired, all of her muscles pleasantly worked, and she was sure she was swimming in a sea of sex-fired endor-phins and dopamine. She'd lost count of her orgasms—it sometimes felt like Ian took her directly from one to the next without losing any sweet momentum.

She frowned at the clothing in her suitcase. She hadn't planned on taking quite so many showers and should have brought more changes of underthings.

Then he came out of the shower that he'd taken after her and Olivia knew that she wasn't actually done with him at all. There was something about his muscled figure and handsome face that woke a fire inside her, no matter how satisfied she thought she was only moments before.

"You are so gorgeous," he said, standing naked in the bathroom door. "I cannot believe you're here with me."

Since they were both naked anyway, it made sense to kiss, which turned to caresses, which turned to sensual strokes, fanning embers of passion that Olivia had thought were banked.

This round was slow and patient, both of them near the capacities of their flesh. She was sore and sensitive, he was responsive to her touches and gradually became hard with her attention. Sore turned to sizzling as he lay her down on the big bed and spread her legs once again. The practice they'd had meant they knew exactly how to tease and tantalize each other to heights again.

The shower that followed was swift and utilitarian, and Olivia was sure that now the weekend had been capped.

She had no regrets.

But they did it once more before dinner, and then again afterwards. Knowing that there was no possible drive back to Nickel City, they shared a bottle of wine with dinner and that last love-making was a blur of pleasure and sensation, full of laughter and more clumsy and silly than any of their earlier rounds.

Afterwards, they lay snuggled together, talking until they were both sober and it was dark and intimate and Olivia wondered how another person's body could feel so much like home, even when they weren't having sex.

CHAPTER 25

Ian forgot to set an alarm, and didn't wake up until checkout time was looming on the bedside clock.

Olivia was still asleep, and he watched her drowse rather than waking her right away, propped up on one arm. Rosy sunlight angled in through the French doors—they had forgotten to draw the drapes again—and it made her look velvety and golden. The perfect treasure for a dragon hoard.

She is beyond value, his dragon agreed. It had been quietly present this whole weekend, Ian thought, focused entirely on Olivia and not on Ian.

Ian remembered Lucy abruptly, and worried for a moment. He wished that he had a cell connection and could check in on her. But instinct didn't suggest that anything was wrong, and he was here with Olivia now, and determined to enjoy every moment of it.

She came awake slowly. The twitch of her hand, a sigh, and her face wrinkled in confusion and regret before her eyes fluttered open.

"Morning," Ian said, bending to kiss her and caress down her nearest arm as she rolled onto her back to look up at him. "Checkout is in about twenty minutes, and I can't afford an extra night's charge if Curtis decides to be a jerk."

"Twenty minutes?" Ian watched her run scheduling in her head as she came fully awake. "Oh, crap."

It was almost worth the rush to watch her roll out of bed and hurry for the bathroom, jiggling and dancing. "I didn't pack last night, oh, wow, how did the bathrobe get here? I smell like rum and Dr. Pepper. Do I have time for a shower?"

"A quick one," Ian said, and he heard her turn on the water as he went to get their suitcases and open them onto the bed. One of the bathrobe belts was still tied to the headboard and Ian chuckled as he undid it. Their last round had been…inventive.

He tapped the last condom out of the box into his suitcase and grinned at Olivia when she came out of the bathroom, fully dressed, with her long, dark hair wet. "I thought I'd been wildly optimistic packing an entire box of these things."

We served her well, his dragon said smugly.

"I'm glad you brought them all, but I also have an implant," Olivia said, unloading the bedside table drawer back into her suitcase. "No danger of Lucy Two."

Ian sucked his breath in with surprise, because the idea of Lucy Two made something flip-flop in his stomach. It wasn't that he was desperate for another child, or that he wasn't stretched to his absolute limit with Lucy One.

It was just that the idea of having a baby with Olivia did something primal to his loins.

Even his very well-used loins.

Olivia didn't seem to notice that he'd stopped packing

and was gazing at her in wonder. She continued to stuff her clothes into her suitcase, pausing to rifle around in the sheets for lost underwear. "I think that's the last lost pair," she said, holding up a bit of lace.

Then she glanced up at him and realized that he was still staring at her hungrily. "You couldn't possibly intend to use that last condom, could you?"

Could he? Physically?

Ian's dragon answered with a surge of power that sent Ian crawling across the bed for her.

He'd gotten deft at getting her clothing off—the bra had been tricky the first few times, but he knew the secrets of its clasp now. And when he slipped his hand down into her hot folds, it didn't take more than a stroke or two of his fingers before she was wet and moaning in his arms.

"There will be a late fee," she warned him.

"I'll mortgage my house," Ian said. "It's a seller's market."

Then he shucked off his own pants and shoved his suitcase to the floor with a crash to lay her down and make good use of the last condom.

～

"Checkout was at eleven," Curtis said pointedly, as Ian handed the keys across the counter in the lobby.

"Oops," Ian said, unapologetically.

Olivia, her face rosy behind her sunglasses, inspected a brochure for horseback tours. "Oh look, they have… ah…legs."

Curtis did not add an extra charge to their bill, but Ian still gulped when he saw it. It wasn't quite mortgage-the-house territory, but it was more than he'd budgeted for. He paid it by credit card before Olivia could see it. There was a payment due for his book when he turned in a draft, that should get him back to square on the card, even if he still had to rent a bouncy house for Lucy's birthday. And he was getting so close to finishing the manuscript, now.

Day care had changed everything.

Then he remembered abruptly that Lucy was *breathing fire* now, and day care might be off the table, and he still hadn't told Olivia any of that, and she probably ought to know, before Lucy went to visit Seltzer and set him on fire.

He had so many questions himself that he wasn't even sure where to start with explaining it to her. Like, why had the fire gone out, when he had only expected it to get worse? And how could Lucy set things on fire if she was a squirrel shifter, and not a dragon at all?

He held the door for Olivia, who was still scarlet-cheeked and pretending that everything was very, very interesting so that they didn't catch each other's gaze and start giggling.

Olivia had changed everything.

Fire-breathing toddler or not, Ian felt like all the disparate parts of his life were starting to fall together, like transparencies that were lining up to make a complete picture.

It even felt like he was better aligned with his dragon now, though the underlying feedback feeling was no less than ever.

Things are more connected than you give credit, his dragon said, with a whiff of the arrogance that always put Ian's back up. *You should tell her, now.*

"I'm almost sorry to go back," Olivia said, slipping into the passenger seat. "My life is going to be so ordinary starting tomorrow. Just boring middle school dramas about boys and quizzes. No more Tiny Paws, no more shifter secrets. Well, except yours, I suppose." She cast him an inviting sideways look and when he didn't answer, she busied herself with something in her purse.

Tell her, his dragon insisted stubbornly.

But the last time that Ian had told someone what he was, it had been the beginning of the end and he wasn't ready to risk losing Olivia.

They talked about nothing as he pulled out of the lodge parking lot, and if was still easy talking to Olivia, he thought that it was a little less *smooth* than it had been on their magical weekend.

"Oh," Ian remembered, halfway back to town. "Did you want to stop for more photos?"

"I had forgotten," Olivia said with a laugh. "No, don't worry about it. We're already running a little behind."

The sky was hazier now; the fires were closer to the area but still safely far away, but the wind had shifted so that most of the smoke was coming this way.

Returning to Nickel City always came with a wave of memories of the times that Ian had come out to the lodge with Roderick during summers between high school. It hadn't changed a lot. It still had the same landmarks, even if the gas station and grocery had changed ownership and the town sprawled a little further out along the highway every year.

"Oh, I know where we are now," Olivia finally said, when they hit the intersection that led into Nickel City proper. "Home sweet home on Crescent Drive."

Ian parked behind his house, then laughed and said, "I should have taken you home, first."

"I think I can walk," Olivia laughed. Ian opened the hatchback for her and she pulled out her haphazardly packed suitcase. "Thanks for the…weekend," she said shyly.

"Thank *you* for the…weekend." Ian wondered if he should kiss her, or if that would lead to needing a new box of condoms. Wanda would be by in less than an hour.

Wanda. Instinct wasn't trying to unhelpfully guide him in any particular direction, and Ian didn't have a bad feeling that he needed to do something desperately, so maybe Lucy had kept her fire-breathing damped down and he'd worried about it for nothing.

"I should go let Seltzer out and scoop his box and see what he threw up on while I was gone," Olivia said lightly. "I left him enough food for a week, but he probably ate it all in one hedonistic day."

Ian had missed his opportunity to kiss Olivia. "It was a good hedonistic weekend all around," he said lightly, and she dragged her wheeled bag behind her up the overgrown path to her back door.

He got his own bag and carried it to his back porch. He could hear Seltzer yowling as Olivia unlocked her door. "Yeah, I'm coming!" she called. "I didn't abandon you!" She turned and waved before she went in.

Ian's house was weirdly quiet. There was no Lucy, no music, no television.

Ian remembered that his phone was still in airplane mode and took it out of his pocket to check his messages.

There were fifteen texts from Wanda.

The last one said, WE HAVE TO TALK.

CHAPTER 26

Tuesday morning, her first day of school, Olivia texted Ian an eggplant and a blowing kiss. *Thanks for a great weekend.*

She had to turn off her phone for class—if only to set a good example for her kids—and thought that it was a little weird that he didn't respond by the end of the school day.

That evening, Lucy didn't drag Ian over to play with Seltzer, even though Olivia sat out in her lawn chair in the back yard, trying to be obvious about the invitation as she worked on the final version of her first school quiz. She agonized over what she should text him next, writing and deleting several flippant lines. She hadn't clearly asked a question, so she shouldn't automatically think he was blowing her off, should she?

We should do it again, she finally texted.

That didn't sound too needy, did it? She only realized after she sent it that it still didn't have an explicit question.

But Ian texted back. *Soon, I hope. Kind of busy right now.*

Kind of busy? Olivia read the eight words over several

times, trying to decide if there was subtle meaning to the brief message.

She decided that she shouldn't read too much into it and texted him back a chili pepper.

There was no response, and eventually Olivia went in to make herself dinner and have a wine cooler to celebrate surviving her first day of middle school without any major mishaps. The next morning, she firmly told herself that she shouldn't blow his lack of answer out of proportion.

After all, she was kind of busy herself.

It was a big culture shock going from Tiny Paws to middle school, but Olivia was surprised how many similarities they had as the week went by.

It was fascinating to watch the awkward tweens interact with each other and trace their behavior to the same desperate need for companionship and connection that the littles had. Their emotional tools were more sophisticated, and their eye makeup (on all genders) was considerably thicker, but they were all still learning to navigate a big world full of big feelings.

The kids jockeyed for favor, scoffed at authority, and absorbed knowledge and affection like sponges, trying to hide behind their cool exteriors and pop-culture mimicry.

They still joked about bodily functions, but at least she no longer had to go with them to the bathroom.

"How'd your first week go?" The principal, Delinda Shaw, was a Black woman with short-cropped hair who looked like she'd win a wrestling match with a polar bear. Upon meeting her, Olivia had immediately wondered if she was a shifter. She'd actually spent most of her first few days looking critically at her students, trying to guess which ones were shifters and what they might be.

Olivia was cleaning up the science lab and she waved

and smiled. "It's easier than day care!" she laughed. Privately, she added, *especially **shifter** day care!*

"We're so happy to have you," Delinda told her.

Olivia wasn't sure what to think of that, except that… she believed the principal. They were happy to have her, and like it had been with Cherry, it may have stemmed from a place of 'any warm body,' but it was already considerably more than that. She'd gotten along well with all the teachers she'd met, and bonded with several of the students already.

Nickel City could be exactly the place for her…except that Ian had been really weirdly distant since their weekend away.

He would answer a texted question if she sent one, but it was completely brief and to the point, no extra chatter, no eggplants. Smiley faces, maybe a thumbs up, but no hearts. When she proposed meeting up, he was vaguely and apologetically busy. He didn't seem to go anywhere, not even to take Lucy to day care, and she heard his fire alarm go off several times, so he was cooking at home. And they saw each other out in the yard, once or twice, but although his wave seemed friendly and they exchanged a distant conversation about the weather and the need for rain, he always immediately had to go.

I think I love you, he'd said. But not a word about it, since then.

Olivia couldn't help but think about her last attempt at a relationship and his sudden coolness triggered every stupid insecurity that she had. Why was he avoiding her? Had it just been a weekend of sex so hot that she had to sit gingerly for a few days…and he was trying to get rid of her now? He hadn't been actively unfriendly or completely ignoring her, but this chilled distance was somehow even worse than that.

It felt like her time at Tiny Paws had been surreal, something from another world altogether, and in the face of an ordinary school, with ordinary children who never once shifted into animals (with or without their clothing).

She sometimes wondered if she had just imagined the whole thing.

CHAPTER 27

When she dropped Lucy off, her lips thin and her eyes accusing, Wanda didn't say a single word about how much trouble the little girl had been. Lucy ran directly for the bathroom, babbling a completely incomprehensible account of her weekend as she went.

"I hope you had a lovely weekend," Wanda said coldly, handing over Lucy's scorched bag. "Convenient that you were out of cell phone range the *entire* time."

Ian started to protest, and give the excuses he'd used with himself—that Lucy had only breathed fire once, it might have been a fluke, she seemed to have put it out, that he didn't know for sure if it would happen again…

He found himself pausing before he spoke, waiting for a confrontation that didn't actually come in his head. His dragon was awake, but not offering unsolicited advice about how to handle the matter. In fact, his dragon seemed to be waiting to see what *Ian* would do. His dragon was mostly thinking about *Olivia.*

How many times had Ian deliberately taken the low

conflict—*doormat*—choice, merely because his dragon was pushing him to be more aggressive and dominant?

You are very stubborn, his dragon observed without judgment.

Ian closed his mouth without trying to grovel and justify why he hadn't given Wanda more warning. He had genuinely tried to tell her what had happened and he didn't have to tolerate being steamrolled, not by anyone. Not even by *himself.*

"It was a great weekend," was all he said, with mild serenity.

That was an understatement. It had been the most amazing weekend of his life, Ian thought. It had been the greatest Dear Penthouse letter in the history of sexy getaways, and Olivia was the spiciest hot tamale that he'd ever unwrapped.

Wanda looked like he'd caught her off balance. She had expected an apology, a little cowering, probably. Surely, this must be all his fault, because he was a *dragon.* Everything between them usually came back to that.

But Ian was done apologizing for what he was, and he was down to the mystery of figuring out *what,* exactly, he was. Because Lucy wasn't a dragon. Ian's dragon was certain that he'd know if she was, and anyway, she was clearly a squirrel shifter.

So this new ability must be because of something else, something from Ian's side of things, and he neither needed nor wanted Wanda along on this particular journey of self-discovery.

"Thanks for taking her this weekend," Ian said mildly, crowding Wanda back towards the door. "We should sit down and go over The Schedule some time soon, but I've really got to get back to work now." He hung up the diaper bag and opened the door for Wanda in an unmistakable gesture. "Drive safe. You'll want to beat the traffic. Lucy, come give your mom a hug goodbye!"

Wanda waited just long enough for Lucy's enthusiastic hug, and then left.

Scorched earth, Ian thought wryly. He'd never wanted things to be contentious, but he was also done being an apologist for things outside of his own control.

But his plan for introspection about his nature and coming clean with Olivia was greatly complicated by Lucy herself.

What started as a simple snack turned into a temper tantrum, complete with nearly setting the kitchen on fire.

It was worse than teething, worse than her pre-shift fits, and the worst of it was how frightened Lucy was of her own powers. She would get herself completely worked up, then blow fire in frustration, then cry because she knew that she'd done the wrong thing, then scream because she didn't know how else to cope with all her strange new sensations.

Ian's de-escalation prowess was put to serious test, and he had to draw on every shred of experience that he had, both as a father, and as a troubled dragon child.

"I know it's hard, baby girl," he told her, cradling a weeping Lucy as he paced the house. He had to draw the curtains, and the fire alarm squawked at regular intervals. She alternated between cuddling desperately close and pushing him violently away.

She was too wound up to sleep that night and Ian spent every moment comforting and consoling her. They snatched a little rest together on the couch near morning, Lucy drowsing on his chest like she hadn't done since she was an infant.

Ian had some hope that morning, as he made them a late breakfast. Lucy was bouncing and full of joyful energy.

But then she caught sight—or other sense—of the flame on the gas stove and freaked completely out. They were back to square one at getting calm and under control again, and the day went basically the way the evening before had gone, testing every limit of Ian's patience and Lucy's lung power.

Olivia texted him a few times, and Ian, one-handed, composed brief, vague messages in return, but when he went to try to call her, desperate to tell her what was going on, he stared instead at the phone and dialed another number.

"Mom," he said to her answering service. "I need you to call me back. It's urgent and I need answers."

If this was something that Lucy had gotten from him, he must have gotten it himself from somewhere.

CHAPTER 28

*I*an's car was parked in the alley. The small branch that had been across his windshield that morning still there, so he hadn't taken Lucy to Tiny Paws that morning. Olivia glanced out her kitchen window at his drawn curtains.

Did he *regret* their weekend? He'd been so distant and secretive since then. She thought about the way that he'd flinched away from the tentative topic of *what he was.* Had he decided that she wasn't actually the one? Had it really only been about sex?

Olivia consoled herself remembering that it had been very, very good sex, but she couldn't help the twinge of uncertainty and dread that came with the memories. She'd come to treasure their flirty friendship, and she'd really hoped that they would be something more. Together.

But it appeared that her worst fears had come into play, and sleeping with Ian had driven him away.

Her last text had gone unanswered, and the curtains over his windows for the first time since she'd moved in seemed like a very unsubtle sign.

A ringing sound startled Olivia and she checked her phone before she identified the sound as a smoke detector, distant and muffled. It was from Ian's house and before she could wonder if she should call him, or maybe the fire department, it turned off.

A cream-colored flash caught her attention from the corner of her eye and Olivia saw Seltzer pounce for the tall grass near the fence. "Oh, no," she said in alarm. "Lucy!"

She ran for the back door, just as Seltzer emerged from the grass with a little squirrel dangling from his mouth. To Olivia's relief, he definitely wasn't in hunting mode, the squirrel was held gently in his teeth, and when he got to the porch, he put her down and let her swarm up his side onto his back before falling over to play with her, his claws sheathed as he batted lightly at her.

The fearless squirrel scrambled all over him, chittering, and when Seltzer trapped her in his paws at last, submitted to being roughly groomed by rolling over and waving tiny paws in the air.

Olivia crouched down next to them. "Lucy," she sighed. "Fingers and feet, sweetie. Fingers and feet." She glanced around, but only Ian's yard had a clear view into hers and there was no one in the quiet alley.

Lucy gave a chatter of complaint and then shifted into a little girl wearing only underpants.

"Did you forget to bring your clothes, Lucy?" Olivia reminded her. She still had trouble wrapping her head around how the whole *bring your clothes with you* thing worked, but she had witnessed enough of it at the day care to know that you had to remember all of your clothes and whatever you were holding or it didn't shift with you. Addison sometimes played *take it with you* games with the older kids that looked very challenging.

Lucy looked down at herself and shook her head. "I

wear this," she explained, as if it made perfect sense to be wearing nothing more.

Maybe it did! It was a hot, dry day and Olivia felt over-dressed in her school clothes. It was entirely possible that Lucy had taken off her dress long before shifting.

Seltzer gave an offended *mrrrt* because he wasn't the center of attention anymore, and nearly knocked Lucy over rubbing his head against her. He was a very large cat and Lucy was a slight girl. Lucy petted him, stroking care-fully from his head to the tip of his glorious tail, and he purred loudly.

"Your dad is probably looking for you," Olivia said, offering her arms.

Lucy smiled and left Seltzer to be picked up. "Daddy," she said happily. "Owiveh an Daddy."

But there was no *Owiveh an Daddy*. Not really. No matter how much Olivia craved his heart, no matter how much she wanted to be a part of their little family.

On cue, she heard Ian calling from the house. "Lucy? Lucy, honey?"

Barefoot, Olivia walked carefully off the porch. Her yard wasn't too treacherous, but there were some rocks she didn't want to step on too hard. She carried Lucy to the fence just as Ian burst out of his back door.

"Lucy, the fire's—" He skidded to a stop on his back porch when he saw Olivia.

"Seltzer caught her again," she told him, pitching her voice to carry. "They were playing."

"Ah good!" Lucy added happily. "Ah good! Sezzer!"

Olivia couldn't identify the expression on his face as Ian came to meet her at the fence. Consternation? Worry? Relief that Lucy was unharmed? Anxiety? Guilt? There were so many *secrets* there. Secrets that he wouldn't tell her.

He also looked like he hadn't slept or showered since the weekend.

The fence was a little too high to comfortably pass Lucy over the top, and just as Olivia was deciding that they were going to have to walk to the end of it, Lucy said, "I hafta go potty!" and shifted into a tiny squirrel that made a lap around Olivia's shoulders, tiny claws pricking through her blouse, and then sprang for the fence. She shimmied down it, and streaked for her house.

"I wish I was half that acrobatic," Olivia said. She wished the fence between them didn't feel so symbolic.

"Thanks," Ian said. "For finding Lucy."

"Seltzer found her," Olivia said.

Ian looked like he was going to start saying something about seven times before Olivia finally asked, "What's going on, Ian?"

Was she being rude? Did it matter? Ian was the one who'd taken her on a sexy weekend getaway and then refused to talk to her.

"It's…really complicated right now," Ian said.

Olivia waited, giving him every chance to try to explain it, and finally prompted him, "Is this about your super secret shift form? Or is it about Wanda? Is there someone else?" She couldn't quite bring herself to ask if he *regretted* their weekend away. It seemed clear that he did.

"No, there's no one else," Ian assured her with flattering speed. "Definitely not Wanda. Definitely not."

He didn't answer the part about the super secret shift form and Olivia felt the bottom of her heart fall out like it was on an uncalibrated elevator.

"You're not letting me in, Ian. I don't want something that's just great sex."

"It's not just sex," Ian said, and Olivia reminded herself that being adorable while blushing was no kind of reason to just forgive him for everything and jump his bones. "Olivia, I really care about you."

Olivia pointed out to herself that he didn't say love when their clothes were staying on.

He went on. "You're the one for me. You're my mate. Instinct says we're supposed to be together."

Olivia felt her chest tighten. If he thought she was the one for her, why was he being so distant?

"You'll tell me that *instinct* says I'm the one, but won't tell me anything else about yourself. I'm supposed to trust you, trust your fancy magical super-sense and just accept that we're going to be *perfect* together, but you won't give me that same level of trust in return."

"It's dangerous—" Ian started, but Olivia was on a tear and she knew that she was going to lose her nerve if she let him try to explain.

"You don't get to decide that for me," she said firmly. "Either we're partners in this, or we're not. And...it's pretty clear that we're not. I'm not so desperate that I want to try to start a relationship on that kind of uneven playing field. I'm sorry, Ian, but are you going to tell me what you are?" Olivia hadn't intended it to sound like an ultimatum, but it hung in the air between them like one.

Ian looked at her with utter despair in his golden eyes and Olivia's only consolation was that he looked as miserable as she felt. "I can't. I don't—"

"Then we're done." Olivia forced herself to say, against all the longing and pain in her chest. "I'm glad we realized it wouldn't work before we both got hurt."

She didn't recognize the lie until the words were out of her mouth.

It was too late for not hurting. Everything about this hurt. Her heart was in one of those medieval torture chambers lined with spikes.

"I'm sorry," she added, just as Lucy hollered from somewhere in their house, "Daaaaaa-ddy! Daaaaaaa-ddy!"

"*I'm* sorry," Ian said swiftly, glancing behind him. "Olivia, I—"

"Don't apologize. You're doing what you think is right and so am I." Olivia knew she was on the brink of tears and the last thing she wanted to do was cry in front of the guy who'd broken her heart. "We're still going to be neighbors, I hope we can still be friends." That was the high ground, right? She was doing exactly the right thing, stopping a doomed relationship in its tracks and leaving space for a polite, professional relationship. At least he hadn't ghosted her. It was better to have closure.

Right?

Ian had that expression on his face like he was fighting with someone in his head. Maybe he was. *Whatever* it was. Lucy was still yelling from the house, sounding more upset now. "Da-ddy! Fah! Fah!"

Ian looked like he was being dragged in two directions. "Look, I want to tell you. I need to tell you, I'm just—there's a lot right now, and I have to—"

"Daaaaaaaaa-ddy!"

Ian bolted.

"I'll see you around," Olivia said to his back, and she turned sharply and made herself walk slowly back to her house instead of bolting the way she wanted to. She didn't let herself turn back to see what Ian did because as soon as her back was to him all of the tears that she hadn't let herself cry in front of him cut loose.

She got inside the door before she really started sobbing, and she reached to shoot the deadbolt home as she slid down the door to sit on the floor. Not that Ian was going to chase her down and break into her house or anything.

Seltzer immediately jumped down from the single kitchen chair and came to investigate her, crawling up into her lap, rubbing his face against hers, and purring like a chainsaw.

He even tolerated Olivia pulling him up into her arms so she could cry into his furry side.

It was so stupid of her, the way that she'd totally fallen for the cute guy next door. This was the first time she was actually glad that she wasn't working at Tiny Paws anymore, so that she wouldn't have to see him at morning drop-off, and she wouldn't have to daydream about what their life together might be like. There was no *together*. There was just a hot weekend of memories and a whole lot of secrets.

She had too much self respect to get into a relationship like that. She was smart and independent.

But smart and independent felt an awful lot like *alone*.

CHAPTER 29

When Olivia broke things off with him, as any sane and normal human being would in the face of his incredible distraction and inattentiveness, Ian had just spent nearly three days being screamed at and pounded on by a tiny, turbulent whirlwind on approximately three total hours of sleep.

And when she asked what he was, he was at a complete loss.

What *was* he?

His dragon was asleep, and where did that leave him? Fragile and human? Why could he still sense fire when their bond was quiet? Ian had always thought it was a lingering side effect of having a dragon inside of him, but he couldn't feel the magical pull of instinct when the dragon slept. Why could he feel this? And how was Lucy, not a dragon at all, able to do *any* of this?

Lucy had managed to scorch her favorite board book, but the fire was out by the time Ian came inside and she crawled into his arms with it and fell asleep.

Was she starting to run out of steam? Ian tried to

remember how her previous growing pains had gone—
when she started shifting it had been a similar process,
impossibly frustrated and fussy for several days right up
until she popped into her squirrel form for the first time.
Then Ian was in for a whole new kind of challenge, trying
to keep her enthusiastic shifting a secret from neighbors.

And now she was...something else. Something more
rare and magical, and it was making Ian reconsider his
entire understanding of *himself*.

He sat with Lucy cuddled in his arms until he was sure
she was entirely under, then stood and carried her to the
bedroom. His whole house smelled of sulphur and smoke.

She went bonelessly into bed and Ian thought about
crawling in after her to try to snatch some sleep himself.

One thought drew him back.

Olivia.

He owed Olivia answers, but he didn't have them
himself.

What *was* he?

Who was he?

Ian remembered trying to pin a name on his dragon at
a very young age. Their voices were distinct in his head, so
he struggled to maintain his own autonomy and his
identity.

Later, with Curtis and Roderick, he'd asked them how
they distinguished their animals from themselves and
they'd been confused.

"I wouldn't be me without my wolf," Roderick said
thoughtfully. "I'd be someone else."

"I can't remember not having my bear," Curtis agreed.
"That would be too weird."

Their animals slept at times, too, but when Ian tried to
pry from them whether they ever had other, unexplainable
magic senses that weren't instinct, things they could tap

into when their animal wasn't there, the weird static charge feedback feeling when it was, they both shrugged and shook their heads. Ian was already having enough trouble fitting in, coming from homeschool and being a mythical animal, that he hadn't pressed the issue, only accepted it as another way he was different, another thing he had to be quiet and secretive about, and not think about too hard.

Ian was staring through the bookshelf, at the spines of a few photo albums, and he drew one of them down. He'd gotten it a box of his father's things when he died. He'd been meaning to get some photos of Lucy printed, to document her growing up, carefully weeding out any photographs that might be incriminating. He hoped that she would always be able to look back and see how much she'd been loved, even if her family wasn't picture book perfect.

Ian flipped through a few pages; there were a few photographs of his parents' wedding, himself as a baby...wearing pink. (They had apparently been expecting a daughter.) His father always looked grim, like he was concentrating. His mother always looked directly at the camera with a practiced smile.

There was a kitchen, their condo in the city. There was a park that Ian was too young to recall.

There was the cabin, where he had some of his happiest memories. He had felt perfectly safe, out in the middle of the private little lake, swimming and shifting and learning to fly with his dragon. The last half of the album was empty. His parents had divorced before he turned eight and his father had died before it could be filled with graduation photos.

Ian turned back several pages as something occurred to him, and frowned at his own scowling image.

He was Lucy's age in that photograph. He had her

same round cheeks and toddler limbs, he couldn't possibly have been older than two, and he was standing on the familiar porch of the wilderness cabin, clinging to the rail.

But they hadn't moved out to the cabin until after he'd become a dragon, after he'd burned down the city apartment.

And he wasn't a dragon until he turned four, he was absolutely sure of that fact.

Had he had powers of fire *before* he was a dragon?

Did I? he demanded inside himself.

I know you needed me, his dragon said, confused and shaken from sleep. It might be older, and wiser, but it sometimes had an uncertain grasp on the passage of days, dismissing linear time as a frail mortal necessity. *I needed you, and you needed me.* It had never been able to be more specific about why it had chosen Ian, though Ian had often asked.

I always thought that you were the reason I lost control, Ian said, trying to pick the memories from the faded recesses of his mind. But if he was two when they moved, and not a dragon when it first happened...

His dragon had always had iron control when it was awake. It was when it slept that Ian feared losing his grip...but he'd always assumed that they were his dragon's powers, and now he suddenly suspected that they weren't.

He plucked his phone from his pocket and realized that he'd never sent the last text he'd typed out to Olivia, pulled away by a Lucy-mergency. It was only half a message: *Sorry I didn't write sooner, some stuff going on, we should...*

He needed to finish the thought, but first, he had to find the answers that they both deserved.

Swiping out of the text app, he browsed to his contacts and pressed on his mother's name.

This message was more curt than the first. "Mom, you

owe me a call. Get back to me now, please. It can't wait any longer."

The house was weirdly quiet, with Lucy sleeping and Ian wondered if he could get Olivia to meet him at the fence to try to tell her what was going on. As he glanced between slats of the kitchen blind, he saw a car pull up in front of their houses and a woman in white rhinestone cowboy boots got out.

Veronica Chase.

She was Olivia's landlady, even if Ian had dodged having her as his, so it wasn't unexpected for her to be there, but it put a crimp on Ian's plan to go beg his way back into Olivia's good graces while Lucy finally napped.

He was staring at his phone again when it rang and he almost dropped it trying to answer. "Mom."

"Ian, darling. Do you need money?"

CHAPTER 30

Olivia pounded a nail into the wall with more fury than skill, skidded the hammer off the head and had to nurse her throbbing thumb for several moments before she could return to the task at hand.

She wasn't sure why she was bothering to decorate.

She hated this house, this neighborhood, this whole town. Her heartbreak made it all look bleak and she hadn't imagined that the smoke was getting thicker; there was an air quality alert warning people not to exert themselves outdoors.

Of course, she couldn't exactly blame that on Ian, like she could the rest of it. There were strict burn bans in place, and the radio in her car was constantly warning about nearby wildfire and which areas were on standby for evacuation.

Seltzer cried at the back door, but when Olivia refused to open it for him, he didn't chew her out the way that he usually would. Instead, he gave her a conversational scold and twined himself around her ankles, trying to climb into her lap when she crouched to pull a framed print out of the box.

Olivia petted him, distracted. It was her favorite photograph once, a macro shot up a mossy log that gave a sense of ancient magic and wonder. But she couldn't look at the photo now without remembering the co-op she thought that she'd belonged to, just like she couldn't look out her kitchen window without a pang of pain.

She wasn't going to be the weepy discarded girlfriend, she just wasn't. She was better than that. She was better than all of them.

The knock on the door made her heart leap. Had Ian followed her after all? Was he here to apologize? To beg her back?

She hadn't decided whether she was going to throw herself into his arms or throw something *at* him when she opened the door, and her disappointment when it wasn't him made her think that she would have taken him back entirely too easily.

"Veronica," she said.

Olivia had thought that Veronica Chase only seemed plastic because of the disconnect of a video interface, but if anything, she was less realistic in person. She had hair that must be sprayed into place with glue, every strand carefully arranged, and she was wearing a tight, low-cut plaid shirt with sparkling buttons. Her white cowboy boots had high heels.

"You said that there was a problem with the stove?" She sounded unimpressed and impatient.

"There were...a couple of problems," Olivia said, wondering how bad her face looked after her crying jag. Maybe Veronica would think the smoke was bothering her. "The front left burner only works on high, like the rheostat is out. The light in the oven is out. Um…I haven't been able to figure out how to turn on the living room fan."

"Lights are consumables," Veronica sniffed. "Not covered under your lease."

Olivia decided it probably wasn't worth arguing that appliance maintenance was covered under the lease, and this was a gray area.

They walked around the house while Olivia pointed out other minor problems, Veronica snapping lazy photographs with her phone. She pointed out that the bare nail that Olivia had put in would need to be plastered over when the lease was up. Seltzer left his perch on the windowsill to come collect his worship due from their visitor.

Veronica nudged him aside with one of her boots. "You won't get your deposit back if the animal damages the carpet," she warned.

Seltzer, undeterred, sidled up and rubbed himself against the rhinestones on the white boots.

Veronica stepped back, and almost tripped over him when he managed to twine himself around behind her.

"Oh, are you a photographer?" Veronica asked.

The framed photo was lying out next to Olivia's camera and telephoto lens.

"Sort of," Olivia said tightly.

"A lot of weird stuff happens around here," Veronica said. Her manner was somehow warmer, all of a sudden, like she was including Olivia in her confidence, and Olivia was immediately suspicious. "Lots of secretive people and strange animals have been spotted in nearby woods. Polar bears, and even more bizarre things. Keep your eyes out, maybe you'll get a lucky shot."

Was she suggesting that Olivia should go out hunting

after Bigfoot...or did she have a clue about the secret shifters living in Nickel City?

Olivia felt the hairs at the back of her neck rise up. She had to protect Lucy, and Ian, and Addison, and all of the kids at the day care...even if she wasn't a part of that inner circle anymore. She was keenly aware of the Tiny Paws magnet on her fridge.

"I'll keep my eyes out," she said, as mildly as she could. "If you could get someone here about the stove? It's not a big problem, but I'd appreciate being able to use that burner again."

Veronica seemed to take the hint, or possibly she saw the magnet, and she left without making any promises.

Seltzer escorted Veronica to the door but didn't try to escape, returning with Olivia to the photo on her unpacked boxes. When she tried to pick it up to hang it, Seltzer stood up and put his paws on it, purring.

Olivia felt like she'd just dodged a bullet, and she wasn't sure why.

She gathered Seltzer into her lap and squeezed him tight.

She wasn't going to give up on the things that she loved, she thought firmly.

"I'll go take new photos," she said firmly. "I don't need Ian for my happiness."

It tasted like a lie in her mouth, but Olivia stood, spilling Seltzer out of her lap, to pack up a day bag with her favorite lenses. She glanced at the card readout on her camera to see if she needed to put a new one in and flipped idly back through a few frames to unexpectedly find the last shot that Ian had taken of her.

He'd been standing very close, and the photo had a soft flattering focus that caught her look of wonder and adoration.

"You're beautiful," he'd told her.

But he'd also told her, "I think I love you," and he'd still been able to just shake her off and shut her out.

Olivia snapped the camera off and tucked it into her camera bag.

She wasn't sure why she'd fallen so hopelessly in love with this guy. Was it because he'd exposed her to an entire supernatural world of sorcery and made her feel like dreams could come true? Was it because she was desperate to belong to someone and wanted to believe that love spells could exist?

But it had all just been completely ephemeral, and now she was on her own again, excluded from the magic and left alone, like always.

Olivia threw her camera bag and a bottle of water into her car and took off, trying not to look at Ian's house as she passed it. She pulled out onto the highway towards the Belle Lake Lodge road.

She didn't know the area around Nickel City very well. There were dozens of roads on her map that wound up into the mountains, and she picked one of them basically at random, hoping to get good photographs of the eerie red skies reflecting on still lakes over dark forests.

It was just the kind of apocalyptic hellscape that she felt inside, so it seemed perfectly fitting.

CHAPTER 31

"You said it was urgent," Ian's mother said. "Do you need money?"

Not urgent enough to call right back, apparently. Ian tried to figure out how many days it had been since he'd left the first message. Two? Three? His mother did everything in her own time. He noticed that she didn't ask about Ian's health, or Lucy's.

"I have questions," Ian said without preamble. He hadn't called to pick a fight, only to get answers. Answers that he should have had long ago. "What am I?"

She was silent for a moment. "I'm not sure what you're aski—"

"Why did my dragon pick me?" Ian asked firmly. "Why not a grown up? Someone older, someone more suited for the job."

"Well, I certainly don't know," his mother said, in that offhanded voice that put Ian's back up as surely as his dragon could. "Maybe he wanted someone young and pliable. Maybe it was because you were..."

Ian held his breath for a moment, waiting for her to finish, but she didn't. "What aren't you telling me?"

You were hot, like me, the dragon said now. It was still largely focused on Olivia, on why they weren't with Olivia, on how they might have failed Olivia, on how they could win Olivia back. It was like having a dog in Ian's head, straining on a leash.

Ian's mother sighed. "I don't really...*know.*"

"You know *something,*" Ian pointed out.

"It was your father's fault," she said.

Ian practiced all of the patience he had learned handling Lucy. "I'm going to need a little more information than that."

"He was...a fire elemental."

"A fire elemental?" Ian was staggered by the idea. He knew about Isadora Larix, of course, but he hadn't considered that there might be other kinds of elementals, let alone that he might be one of them.

"A powerful magical being with control over fire," his mother explained, as if that was the part Ian might not understand. "Well, mostly he had control. You did test his patience at times." She never failed to remind him what a difficult child he'd been.

"I'm a *fire elemental?* Didn't you think that was the kind of thing I needed to *know?*"

"I'm sure I don't know that much *about* it," his mother said carelessly. "It's from your father's blood, not mine. And we didn't think you could *do* anything after you became a dragon. The creature's powers were much more powerful than yours and he seemed to cancel out your elemental talents."

"Having a dragon who could damp me down was not exactly helpful for my development," Ian said furiously, to both his mother and the dragon steaming in his head. "I never learned to control this power by myself, and now I have to figure out how to teach it to my daughter."

"Is Lucy…?" It was the first time in the whole conversation that she seemed genuinely interested.

"Yes, Mom, Lucy is now breathing fire. You've missed all *kinds* of milestones."

"There's no reason to be huffy with me," she scolded him.

Ian bit back an acid reply and took a deep breath that smelled like fire. "Is there anyone on Dad's side of the family that I can get in touch with? Someone that might have some *answers* for me?"

"I have no contact with them," his mother said dismissively. "Your father was never close with his family and we never met."

"Well, if you think of anything useful, give me a call." Ian guessed that he couldn't consider their conversation a complete dead-end, even if the revelation that he was a *fire elemental* came without the backup of any information that was actually helpful.

"I will," she promised. "Ian…"

"Yeah?" Ian had already pulled the phone from his ear, ready to hang it up, and he returned it.

"How old is Lucy now? Three?"

"She's turning two next month," Ian said.

"I may send her a gift," his mother said hesitantly, like she was uncertain how it would be received.

"That would be great. Thanks." Ian did hang up then, and he stared at the phone for a moment. Dammit, he still needed to schedule Lucy's birthday party. Where did you even *get* a bouncy house?

Ian's dragon was anxious in the back of his head, waiting for a pause in Ian's thoughts. *I did not intend any unkindness,* it said. Ian could not mistake its sincerity. He'd never doubted his dragon's big heart or basic goodness. *I was not consciously damping down your natural gifts.*

I know you didn't mean to be hard on me, Ian said wearily. *But I was four. I didn't have the tools to figure out who I was, to be myself without you. We were never partners, not like shifters are, growing up with each other. You were always the one with all the answers, the older, wiser, stronger one.*

I never thought of you as weak, his dragon said gently.

You never thought of me as strong, Ian pointed out. *I have always been less than you. A frail human that you needed as a mundane vessel, never your caliber of power or intelligence. And you never stopped seeing me as that child, because you didn't grow, and you never noticed that I did.*

Ian gazed at Lucy, who was stacking her blocks taller and taller. They toppled down and she made a babble of outrage. "No!" she protested. "No!" Smoke curled from around her mouth and her red hair took a shimmer of sparks.

"No fire," Ian cautioned. "We do it without fire. You can't take fire back." Except that...maybe they could? What did he know about being an elemental? Who could he ask?

He didn't offer to help Lucy, letting her work through her frustration and start stacking the blocks once more with determination as the smoke ebbed away and her hair returned to its original rusty red. "Remember, blocks falling down are half the fun. Never cry when you can laugh!"

His dragon watched the exchange in wonder and chagrin.

Why did you never tell me this before? his dragon asked gruffly. *How you felt about my control.*

I didn't know it to say, Ian confessed, honest in exhaustion. *I didn't want to resent you and didn't know how to approach you with my feelings. I thought you must know them and not care, or that you'd never see me as an equal, so what was the point. The easiest thing was just to go along, to pick my battles.*

I weary of battle, his dragon said.

Yes, Ian agreed. **Yes.** He was so tired of being in conflict with half of himself.

You should have said something much sooner, his dragon said firmly.

Don't make this my fault, Ian warned, tasting smoke in his own mouth.

I did not intend to, his dragon said. *I am sorry for my role and I perceive it clearly now. I did not see that our partnership had changed, though it should have been obvious to me that it must. I grew…complacent in my ways and did not acknowledge your qualities or contributions. I forgot that humans change so quickly, in the scope of things, and I made assumptions that hurt us both.*

It was a noble apology, and Ian could not for a moment doubt the sincerity or depth of it.

His dragon's next words rocked Ian back on his heels. *You are a worthy partner. I regret that I failed to make that clear to you sooner. I do not regret choosing you. Not ever.*

I don't regret being chosen, Ian said, feeling like his heart had become suddenly unclouded. It was the truth. He loved being a dragon. He loved the power and the wisdom that his dragon brought to him, the feeling of fire in his soul.

Even if some of that had been in his own soul all along.

Can we go to Olivia now? his dragon asked, like a dog at a bone. *Can we fix this together? Now?*

Together really was the only way that they were going to fix it. If he wanted answers about being an elemental, he would have to go to an elemental for them—and he only knew one of those. Ian would visit Isadora Larix, armed with his new awareness, and see what he could learn from another elemental about what he was. And he would tell Olivia everything.

Just then, instinct rose up from a nagging pull to a siren of alarm and both Ian and his dragon rose in fear and dread.

Olivia was in danger, now! *There! Danger! Distress!*

CHAPTER 32

Olivia remembered that cell data service in the narrow winding valley would be disrupted, but had trusted that the basic GPS service was somewhat more thorough, and that her phone would tell her where she was and how to get back into town.

She hadn't remembered that her phone would grind through its limited charge searching for the cell service when she forgot to put it into airplane mode.

She discovered that the phone was dead the same moment that she realized she was hopelessly lost. She had pulled over to explore a little side road, but the smoke seemed to descend, thicker than ever before, and when she got back to the main road, the visibility was so awful that she wasn't even sure she was at the main road.

In fact, the further she got, the more sure she was that she'd gotten turned around somewhere and was on another side road. Nothing was familiar. There were no signs, and no other cars, just scrubby trees, winding canyons, dusty roads, and smoke.

She pulled over at an intersection to search the car for

a charging cable so that she could find her way back to the highway and when she opened her door, she realized that the terrible hungry sound she was hearing over the sound of her car's engine was fire.

Very nearby fire.

Hands trembling, she returned to her car. There was fine gray ash falling over her and the smoke was stinging her eyes and making her lungs strain.

She was such an idiot. She was one of those storm chasers that got stupidly caught up in an actual tornado. Her legacy would be a melted camera with a few awful photographs of reddish pea soup fog. It wasn't worth it.

Fighting back her terror, she got back into her car and tried to figure out which way to go.

Ash scraped under the windshield wipers as she tried to clear it from her window but it didn't help her visibility until the smoke abruptly lifted and Olivia had a moment of hope.

That was when she realized that the forested mountainside that she could see just across the gorge was licked in flames. She tried to understand the scale of it; those trees were tall, but the fire was taller, and it was heading towards the road before her.

She had to try to get out of here, a circumstance that would have been greatly helped by knowing that she was going in the right direction. The roads were so twisty, the compass in her car didn't help her because she knew that she needed to go generally south, and her options were west and east.

The longer she delayed, trying to remember the direction that she'd come from, searching for anything resembling a landmark in the smoky soup, the more likely she was to be trapped here and caught in the fire itself.

It felt muggy, but not as hot as Olivia expected, given

her proximity to the fire. She was used to sweltering southern summers, and this wasn't that unpleasant. That would change, she guessed, as it got closer to her. It was probably pretty painful, dying in a fire. Already, it was so smoky that her breaths felt laborious.

Should she stay in the car? Try to outrun the fire? (Which way?!)

Instinct would have been of great help right now, Olivia thought, grinding her teeth in frustration.

It just figured that magic was real and *she* didn't have any.

Going felt better than staying, so Olivia picked a direction at random and drove, slower than she wanted to because the visibility was so wretched that she could barely make out the shoulder of the road. At least it hid the terrible sight of the fire on the opposite ridge again.

The air was thick and cloying. Olivia coughed and then couldn't stop.

She should be breathing through something, Olivia remembered, from distant fire safety classes in elementary school. A handkerchief, or… Olivia reached blindly into the backseat and found the school rally scarf that she could tie over her face. Did her car's air conditioning system help? Should she *stay* in her car, or would that just cook her like a solar oven?

She wasn't sure what part of her difficulty breathing now was from the smoke, what was from trying to suck air through her scarf, and what was sheer panic, threatening to crush her lungs from the inside. She got the coughing under control by sheer will, but the terror continued to swell.

Just when she was ready to pull the car over and have a full blown panic attack, she saw a sudden dark shape come out of the smoke like a spaceship parting clouds in a high budget science fiction movie. She stomped on the brakes, skidding on the gravel, and the car came to a rest in front of a huge, sinuous form with outstretched wings, smoke swirling around it like one of her airflow science experiments.

For a long moment, she did nothing but stare over her steering wheel as the creature's head slowly lowered and looked at her with glowing golden eyes.

It was a dragon, she recognized, over her pounding heart and gasping breath.

It was a dragon straight out of legend, with lapping scales that caught what light there was like cut jewels, patterned in shades of gold and bronze. Its wingspan was twice the width of the road, before it folded them and settled them against its shimmering back.

Its head was wedge-shaped, with nostrils at the end of long, wicked snout, and a snake-like neck that joined muscular shoulders. It was like something out of a medieval illustration—and somehow not at all like that, slim and delicate like a bird.

Olivia discovered that she hadn't put the car in park when it began to roll forward as her foot came off the brake that it had been jammed down on and it took her a few tries to get it in the parking gear, she was shaking so badly. She turned off the car altogether, sure she shouldn't be trying to drive it now anyway.

There was a dragon in the road in front of her.

A real, breathing, flying dragon, with whirling golden eyes. Olivia's thoughts finally broke through her fright and all the little pieces and parts fell into place. It was *Ian*.

*I*an knew where Olivia was, his understanding of instinct's message, for once, completely clear.

He didn't need vision, which was fortunate, because the whole valley was socked in with dense smoke, the road beneath them only visible at all in stuttering intervals.

There, go, fly, faster! For once, he was the one directing *his* dragon, urging them through the murk. He didn't particularly enjoy flying, but he was grateful to have wings; he never would have made it to her in time driving a car or running on four feet.

He saw the fire before he saw her car, and felt a jolt of terror and…recognition?

He remembered Isadora's snarling attack. *You're dangerous.*

The fire felt familiar, because he was fire.

Ian swooped closer to the road and found Olivia's car creeping through the smoke in his direction. He back-winged down in front of her, realizing that this meant she would know what he really was. Or at least, part of it.

She skidded to a stop and stared through her gritty

windshield at him. She had a scarf over her face, and her eyes above it looked red.

Smoke, or tears? Ian wondered. He'd broken her heart and his own along with it. Guilt swamped him and he shifted to run on human legs to the side of her car so he could wrench open the door and try to draw her out.

There was a bad moment when neither of them could figure out seatbelts or how to operate them, and then Olivia was falling out of her car into his arms, weeping. "I didn't know which way to go!" she sobbed into his chest. "And you're a *dragon*! You're a *dragon*!" She beat at him weakly.

"I'm a dragon," Ian agreed, holding her tight. "And I should have just told you, but I'm apparently an *idiot* dragon."

He waited for his dragon to agree, but there was only worry there. *Fire, behind us,* the dragon warned. *Save her!*

There was no way left to drive out, and Olivia was too much for him to carry safely out by wing. If she had kept going, she would have driven right into the fire crossing the road.

He didn't want to tell her that.

But he recognized in dismay that keeping things from her had nearly destroyed their chances together. He didn't want to be that person with *any* secrets. "We aren't safe here," he told her. "The fire is all around now." He wasn't going to pretend that he knew what to do next.

The fire was noisy, a rushing noise like a roaring stream mixed with wind and crackling trees. The air felt thick in his lungs.

Can we make a firebreak? Ian asked. He had only the foggiest notion what a firebreak even was, but he knew that it was part of firefighting. If there was nothing left to burn, the fire couldn't travel towards them.

His dragon, to his surprise, felt full of panic, even as Ian felt an eerie calm settle over him. *There is too much fire, we can't protect her!* his dragon wailed.

Ian let go of Olivia, whose sobs had faded into hoarse coughs, and walked to the edge of the road. Maybe he could stop the fire.

*We only **make** fire,* his dragon protested. *What are you doing?*

***You** only make fire. I **control** fire,* Ian replied, sure of something for the first time in his life.

Ian was remembering Lucy, her unexpected fire breathing and her *direction* of the flame that she'd made. She had put out her first careless fire, and none of her subsequent fires, as alarming as they were, had posed any danger.

Controlling fire once it was released wasn't a thing that a dragon could do…

Because she *wasn't* a dragon. She was a squirrel shifter, like her mother. But she was also a fire elemental, like her father, and her father's father.

You told me that you were attracted to come and be a part of me when I was young because I felt hot, like you, Ian told his dragon. *I had fire before you. I **was** fire before you.*

His dragon was silent.

You kept me from using my gifts because they scared me, but they were always still here. I thought that all of the things I could do were because of you, but some of them were mine all along.

Ian reached a hand to the smoldering grass in the nearest ditch and it swelled up into a column of flame that stretched for the sky and pierced up through the smoke like a sword.

Olivia gave a cry of alarm, holding her scarf close over her mouth.

"It's okay!" Ian assured her, and then he brought his

hand down and collapsed the inferno into nothing, fanning away from them in a rush of cooling, clearing air from above.

"Did you put it out?" Olivia asked in awe. "Can you do that?"

Could he?

"Ian?"

"Hang on a moment…I'm not really sure what I'm doing."

Ian had his eyes closed now, trying to figure out the scope and size of the fire around them. It stretched beyond the ridge, down the valley, in an irregular wedge back towards Belle Lake Lodge.

Ian had always been able to sense fire. He'd been able to tell when neighbors had fires going in fireplaces, when someone three blocks over had a burnpile, when anyone nearby was smoking or burning sage. Fire season was like being covered in hives sometimes, he could feel it from a hundred miles away when it was strong.

Even when his dragon was sleeping.

He'd assumed that it was some kind of a residue of having a dragon within him, that maybe he was particularly sensitive to the smell of smoke, and he'd been too young to remember before that, when he was only an elemental.

Ian tried to focus on the here and now.

He could control a ditch of small flame and make party tricks with little columns, but there was so much active fire here, spread so far. Could he stop enough to get them out? Could he stop it *all?*

Just as Ian reluctantly decided it was beyond his strength, his dragon offered, *It is not beyond mine.*

Together? Ian asked in wonder. Could they do it together?

I could not do it without you, his dragon said humbly. *You could not do it without me. Together, we are more.*

Ian sucked in a breath and concentrated, starting with the closest patch of fire. He thought about it until he could feel it, like he was holding his hand in a great bowl of half-set Jell-o, and when he imagined moving his fingers, he could feel the drag of it against him.

Then his dragon joined him, and the rush of power was like nothing Ian had ever felt.

"Ian?" Olivia was standing close beside him, and he hadn't warned her what he was attempting to do.

He should tell her more, Ian thought, feeling guilty. He should tell her everything, always, because she was his other half and his heart. Instinct was telling him that they would be complete together.

But for the moment, he couldn't speak at all, already sending himself out into the wildfire that was closing in on them.

He could feel it, creeping towards the Belle Lake Lodge, threatening to roar through the trees towards Nickel City itself. It had been weeks since there was rain, and the entire forest was tinderbox dry. The feral fire was hungry for it. No wonder Isadora was afraid and angry.

Ian had braced for painful heat, for burning, but it was a lapping welcome. This was his element, he was fire. As hard as he'd tried to fight it, as much as he'd tried to deny this part of his nature, or blame it on his dragon, he had a soul of flame and the wildfire was his kin.

And now that he understood it?

He could control it.

With the strength of his dragon behind him, he could tame the heat, bring it to heel, and soothe it down to smoldering nothing. Yard by yard, mile by mile, he slowly folded it down, turning it to ashes and dying embers. It was the work of a hundred hours by a hundred firefighters and gallons of water and suppressant, done with the will of his mind and his dragon.

He lost his sense of Olivia beside him, his understanding of his feet on the ground. He was everywhere and everything, like fire itself, until it finally died to nothing.

It sleeps, his dragon said, sounding weary in his head. Its presence was starting to fade. *I must rest.*

I could not have done that without you, Ian said, in an unconscious echo of his dragon's earlier words. He felt weak, and realized as he came back to himself that Olivia was holding him upright. His legs were rubbery and he wasn't sure what was smoke and what was his vision smearing with exhaustion.

"Ian, Ian?" Olivia was asking in alarm. "Ian, are you all right?" She was trying to tie the scarf over his face. The air was still thick and impenetrable with smoke but Ian realized that the staticky crackle of the fire was gone. "Ian!"

In the silence that the fire's roar left behind, Ian could hear sirens and distant tires on gravel. A Montana DNRC wildlands team must have been called to fight the fire.

"Ian?" Her voice was hoarse and raw.

"I'm okay," he rasped. More importantly, "*You're* okay. The fire is out. I put it to sleep."

"What did you do?" she choked. "How did you do it?"

"I'll tell you everything this time," Ian promised. His vision was fading and Olivia's dear face was clouding over. "I should have before. Everything."

He didn't remember collapsing.

CHAPTER 34

*I*an weighed a great deal more than Olivia was able to keep upright when he finally lost consciousness, and she fell over backwards with him wrapped in her arms.

"Ow," she said. The road here was mostly dust, and it might have been worse on gravel, but it was not at all comfortable and she knew that she was going to have impressive bruises on her ass.

Ian was still breathing and when Olivia put trembling fingers to his throat, his heartbeat seemed strong. Whatever he'd done, however he'd stopped the fire, it had taken every ounce of his power, but he wasn't dead. Olivia wanted to weep, but felt too dried out to do so.

Somewhere nearby, she could hear sirens coming, climbing the mountain towards them.

Great. He would save her from a wildfire in order to be run over in the middle of the road by a fire truck that couldn't see them through the lingering smoke. Olivia dragged Ian towards the ditch, wincing with every rock that she had to struggle to get him over. "Sorry," she said to his unresponsive body. When she felt that they were safely off far enough, she gathered his head into her lap and wished she'd found a rock to prop herself up on, because she didn't have a lot of energy left herself and even sitting upright seemed like a lot of work. Her lungs felt like they were filled with molasses.

Olivia had wondered if Ian wasn't something that he felt was embarrassing. A flamingo, maybe, or a skunk? A mosquito, maybe? She thought that his reluctance to talk about his shift form might be because he was ashamed of it. In all of her ideas and imagining, *dragon* hadn't so much as crossed her mind.

She laughed, but that made her cough. Tara, one of the little girls at Tiny Paws, was a kirin, a kind of Chinese unicorn, but Olivia still hadn't imagined that dragons might be real. It was no real surprise that Ian hadn't been able to show her his form. There was no hiding that in a suburban backyard; dragon-Ian could probably look right over the top of either of their houses, let alone their fences.

The sirens were close now, and Olivia thought she probably ought to stand up and try to wave the firetruck down, but Ian was heavy in her lap, so she just waved her arms as soon as she saw them coming through the smoke.

The wildlands trucks weren't like the long red fire engines she was used to, they were squat and efficient, more suited for bad roads and tight turns. They were painted bright yellow, and the men that spilled out when they skidded to a stop were also dressed in yellow. Olivia supposed that made them easy to spot through thick smoke.

"Are you hurt?" the first man to reach her asked, dropping to his knees beside them to inspect Ian.

"No," Olivia said hoarsely. "No, I'm okay…he just…"

exhausted himself magically putting out a forest fire. How did you explain that? How did you explain any of this? All she could do was shrug.

The man gave her a piercing and suspicious look as the next man, a medic with dark hair and a trimmed beard, crouched down with a first aid kit at hand. His look seemed slightly more knowing. Were any of these firefighters shifters? Did they recognize Ian as one of them? Olivia wondered if she would always feel a little left out now that she knew about magic.

She was going to have to get over that if she was going to have a boyfriend who was a dragon with a daughter who was a squirrel.

And Olivia realized wearily that she didn't want anything in the world more than she wanted that.

"I don't get it," one of the yellow-clad men was saying, puzzling over a tablet. "Satellite is showing no active fire anywhere near here. A few minutes ago, this whole area was hot, now there's nothing for miles."

"I don't hear any fire, either," another observed. "Eerie."

"In this wind, it ought to be building up, not dying down," another suggested.

"It's like someone knew we were coming and turned the whole thing off," someone joked.

The bearded man with the first aid kit looked hard at Ian and then quizzically at Olivia.

"Plenty of smoke, still." The first man had finished his inspection of Ian and turned to check Olivia over, taking her pulse and checking her pupils, feeling her head for injury. She tried not to giggle. Hitting her head might actually explain some of what she had seen. "Let's get them both some oxygen."

Olivia tried half-heartedly to protest, then obediently

sucked in the clean air that was pressed to her. Her lungs hurt. The medic felt the back of Ian's head for injuries, then strapped a mask to his face as well. He was unresponsive and Olivia felt her heart drop out of her chest.

"You've both breathed a lot of smoke," the first man said. "We can give you a ride back to town."

"My car," Olivia tried to say, around the oxygen bag. She gestured back in the direction that she thought she'd left her car. She was all turned around in the smoke again.

"Is it off the road?" the dark-haired man wanted to know.

Olivia shook her head. "The keys are in it."

"You'll probably be alright to drive pretty soon, we'll just move it off to the side so it's not in our way. Johnson! Fletcher!" The medic had the kind of tone that everyone obeyed and two of the yellow-suited young men jogged off into the murk.

The first man exchanged a complicated look with him and went to herd the remaining fire fighters back out of earshot.

The medic seemed to gather himself, glancing around to determine that everyone around them was occupied in some manner, and then he put his hand on Ian's chest.

Olivia felt Ian jolt in her arms, like he'd just gotten shocked by electric paddles, and he drew in a sharp, deep breath.

"Owiveah," he managed, sounding through the oxygen mask just like Lucy trying to say her name.

"He'll be okay in just a minute," the medic said. "I'm Becket."

It took Olivia a moment to recognize that he hadn't said *bucket*. She managed not to giggle hysterically.

"I'm Olivia," she replied. "This is Ian." He was going to live.

"Owivea," Ian said again.

It was everything Olivia could do not to bend her head over him and weep.

*J*an felt like he'd been locked in a gym and forced to use every weight machine on maximum for an entire day. Every muscle in his body ached. His head ached. His heart ached. Parts of his brain that he hadn't even realized he *had* ached. Even instinct seemed to throb. The feedback feeling was more painful than ever, like his brain was raw.

His dragon was there, barely. He was as exhausted as Ian was, but clinging again to consciousness.

There was a bag over his face, muffling his words and when he tried to remove it, a dark-haired man in a yellow firesuit stopped him. He could feel a flash of instinct from him through his agony. This man was the one who'd brought him back to consciousness, Ian thought, though he couldn't identify exactly what he was or how he'd done it.

"Olivia?" he said. Had she been hurt? Had he managed to stop the fire? Had the smoke been too bad for her to handle? "Olivia?" He had to know she was okay.

Before he could struggle in earnest with the stranger to sit up, Olivia was there, pressing down on his shoulder. She had a mask of her own, but no one stopped her when she pulled it off. "Ian! Ian, are you alright?"

Ian didn't need the oxygen; the smoke didn't bother his lungs.

He exchanged a long, knowing look with the EMT, then took Olivia's hand into his own so that he could sit. "I don't need this," he said, taking off the mask. The EMT's name tag said *Becket.*

Becket didn't challenge him. "You put the fire out," he observed. "It cost you a great deal of energy."

Olivia looked from one of them to the other, a look of resignation on her sooty face. Did she feel left out? She said she hated that more than anything, and he'd had to shut her away at the worst possible time.

"It almost cost me more than that," Ian said wryly. He didn't attempt to deny who he was or what he'd done. He struggled up to his feet, and Olivia stood with him. He wasn't sure which of them was more help to the other.

"This must be your mate," Becket observed, winking at Olivia. "Nice to meet you both."

Olivia went pale beneath the grime on her cheeks.

"She's my mate," Ian said firmly. "If she'll have me."

His dragon had fallen into spent slumber, satisfied that they were safe, but Ian didn't need his connection to instinct to tell him that she was the one. His heart had all the faith he needed.

"This is a lot," Olivia said in a very small, smoky voice.

Becket cleared his throat. "You guys are both fine to go, as long as you take him directly home. Rest will do him a world of good, and if you ever need any…specialized medical services, you can call me directly." He slipped a card to each of them, and Ian glanced at his to find a simple graphic design with four different pawprints and a blocky "Early Shift Medical Services" with a phone number. "Your car is a short distance back that way. Drive slow on your way out, and remember…" He winked at Ian. "Only you can prevent forest fires. Apparently."

He took the oxygen masks and first aid kit back to the looming shape of the fire truck, where the rest of the rescue crew was still checking their reports and marveling over the fact that there was no further fire in the area.

"I should have told you what I was a lot sooner," Ian said quietly. "I should have *known* what I was a lot sooner."

"You didn't know?" Olivia said. Her brows were knit in confusion.

"I'm a dragon shifter," Ian said. "But I'm something more, too, and so is Lucy. We're elementals, like Isadora. But where she is about life, about trees and plants, we are fire."

"Your smoke alarm *has* been going off an awful lot lately," Olivia observed.

Ian winced. "Yeah, I should probably just disconnect those until Lucy has better control. Until *I* have better control."

Olivia shook her head. "I noticed that my hair smelled a lot like smoke when she'd been riding around on my shoulder for very long. I just assumed that it was from the wildfires, but it didn't happen so much when she missed day care or I didn't work."

Ian couldn't resist the smudge on her cheek any longer and she didn't flinch away when he used the end of her scarf to wipe it off. "I am so sorry. I should have trusted you, and told you what I did know from the very begin-ning." The smudge was stubborn and Ian had to keep himself from licking her scarf to scrub it off harder like he might have with Lucy.

"I see why you wouldn't," Olivia said with a shrug of one shoulder. "You had Lucy to think of."

"It was still wrong," Ian said, setting his jaw. "I knew that you were safe to tell anything to and I didn't. That was my failure."

Olivia's whole face softened. "I can't really…blame you."

"That does not make it okay and I won't do it again," Ian promised with his whole heart. "I won't keep things from you. No matter how sticky or complicated, I want you to be my partner in all things."

Olivia's eyes crinkled with humor. "All things? Because there are some things you can keep to yourself," she teased. "I was happy to leave the open bathroom doors behind at Tiny Paws."

"I promise to close the bathroom door," Ian laughed, and he had to kiss Olivia then, taking her dirty face in both hands.

Her kiss in return was deep and soft, broken off rather more quickly that Ian would have liked with her cough.

"We should get home," he said. "I left Lucy at Tiny Paws without an appointment and sort of yelled at Cherry that she could breathe fire now on my way out and I'm probably going to have to pay for some damages."

"Oh, yeah, Cherry might have a few choice words about that," Olivia chuckled weakly. "The kind of words you can't say at day care."

They were stumbling along together, faithfully following the edge of the road, and Olivia's car rather suddenly emerged from the murk.

"What does this mean?" Olivia asked as she started the car. "I mean, where are we now, you and I?"

"The middle of nowhere Montana in a bank of smoke?" Ian buckled his belt and wondered if it would be inconsiderate to tip the seat back and try to sleep on the way back to town. He still felt rather run-over and bushed.

But they ended up talking on the drive and Ian didn't regret a word of it. It was the way they had talked on their magical lodge vacation, except that he didn't hesitate at the end of a conversation and run away. He told her *why* his parents had moved him out to the middle of nowhere and kept his powers a secret, including all the parts that he knew now that had been opaque to a four-year-old boy, and all the parts he hadn't remembered in order. He talked frankly about the power struggle he'd had with his grown-up dragon, the way it felt like it had wrecked his marriage.

"I don't know if Wanda hated it more that I didn't think I had full control of my dragon or that I was something more special than her. She was…so smug when Lucy turned out to be a squirrel, like her blood was *stronger* than mine." Ian gave a dry chuckle.

"But your dragon isn't like the shifter forms that the kids at Tiny Paws have," Olivia observed. "It was never a baby like you were. Why did it choose you?"

Ian considered. "Maybe because I needed it. I was out of my depth with my powers. My parents were out of their depth with me. I desperately needed guidance."

"Maybe that was part of it." Olivia turned on the wipers and fluid, trying to wipe the scum from the windshield. It didn't help the visibility much. "Maybe a whole lot of things had to happen just right to get to this point, where we were meant to be."

"You think that things happen for a reason?"

She glanced away from the smoked-in road to meet his gaze. "Don't you? After all of this?"

Ian thought about his chances of saving Olivia if he hadn't been a dragon, the probability of her moving in next door, the likelihood of a daughter like Lucy that completed his heart without the heartbreak of Wanda.

Every little part of his life had come together to put him on this path.

Elementals didn't feel magical instinct like shifters did, but even with his dragon in exhausted unconsciousness, he knew that everything was *right*. He was exactly where he needed to be for perfect happiness.

It was weird being on this side of the Tiny Paws doors and Olivia self-consciously straightened her hair for the camera. It buzzed open after just a few moments and Addison was waiting at the gate for her when she got her shoes off, Amy bouncing in her arms in human form.

"Are you okay?" Addison asked anxiously, raking her gaze down her.

Olivia had washed her face when she dropped Ian off, but she was still dressed in sooty clothes and she probably smelled like a campfire. "Yeah," she said with a hiccup of a laugh. "It's…well, it was quite an adventure. Nearly got trapped by a wildfire. The EMT let us go, but Ian's pretty wiped out, so I dropped him at his house and told him I'd pick up Lucy. If that's alright?" Doubt suddenly stabbed at her. Ian had previously made it clear it was okay for Olivia to pick his daughter up, but that had been when she worked there. Would Addison and Cherry toe a hard line on authorizations, now that she didn't? Had she said too much about Ian's role in her rescue?

"No," Addison said firmly. "I meant, are you *okay*? You haven't answered my texts. In like a week."

Had it been that long? Olivia hadn't known what to say to Addison's first few messages and had marked them as read without responding, too heartbroken to pursue them then. She'd never gotten back to answering, and had somehow assumed that breaking things off with Ian meant that she'd been cut off from the shifter community. She didn't work at Tiny Paws anymore, and surely she had only been barely tolerated, as a human. Had Addison missed her? Worried about her? Olivia felt tears gather in her eyes.

"Don't look like that!" Addison said at once, as Amy, picking up on the mood, began to cry in earnest. "Come on back, I've got some animal crackers and a juice box. Sit down in the story circle and tell me all about it, honey."

Addison never seemed pushy, but she was also absolutely impossible to resist. Olivia obediently did as she said, the crunch of the animal crackers helping the hollow in her empty stomach and the juice drink doing wonders for her blood sugar as she sat in the bean bags and stuffies. Lucy caught sight of her at once and dashed over to climb into her lap, a comforting and cuddly weight that Olivia had desperately missed this past week.

Olivia went backwards through the story, telling Addison about their grueling fire ordeal, her flight into the fire to take ill-considered photos, her awful breakup with Ian, the weekend at Belle Lake Lodge, details carefully glossed over with knowing smiles given their tiny, if inattentive, audience. The only thing she didn't tell Addison was what Ian really was.

Then Lucy made some of his secrets a moot point when Amy tried to take a stuffed animal that she was playing with, prompting a jet of angry flame that lit the animal in question on fire.

It went out at once, though Olivia wasn't sure if it was because of the fire-resistant nature of the toy or if Lucy herself had controlled it the way that Ian had learned that he could. The little girl was certainly aghast at what she'd done, and she firmly gave the scorched stuffy to Amy and climbed back into Olivia's lap to press her head into Olivia's armpit in abject shame. Olivia automatically soothed her and stroked her red hair.

"Ian warned us about that when he dropped her off," Addison said, clearly stunned. "I…didn't really believe it." She shook herself and ate another animal cracker. "Well, that's a fun wrinkle. I'll talk to Cherry about some more fire extinguishers."

"I'm sorry," Olivia said wearily. "I'm so sorry."

"Because Lucy can breathe fire? That's hardly your responsibility."

"For not responding to your texts," Olivia explained. "For not reaching out. I didn't think… If I wasn't with Ian, I didn't know if you'd still want…"

Addison looked at her with wry sympathy. "Did you really think that we were only friends because you were in some kind of maybe-maybe-not relationship with Ian? Did you think I'd ditch you because you didn't work here any more?"

"I guess maybe I did," Olivia confessed. As hard as it felt to think she'd lost Ian, it was a hundred times worse because she'd dragged a whole lot of other emotional baggage with her and cut off the other people who cared about her. She'd been sure she'd lost everything again. "I'm not a shifter."

"You're not a shifter," Addison said firmly. "Cherry's not a shifter. My cousin Wendy isn't a shifter. I'm not some kind of…supernatural elitist, Olivia. We've been thrown up on by the same babies. We've shopped the same terrifying garage sales. I like you for you, not for who you're dating or what kind of magic you have."

Olivia felt like a band around her chest had released. She didn't have instinct to tell her if she was going in the right direction, but she didn't need it.

Right now, the right direction was back to Ian, with a very subdued and smoke-scented Lucy.

CHAPTER 37

*P*ine needles and gravel crunched underneath Ian's feet.

He had the trail to Isadora's tree to himself. It wasn't a second Thursday, so he'd parked off the road and hopped the gate, noticing as he did that it wasn't actually locked. A squirrel somewhere distant gave an alarm, and he thought of Lucy. Olivia had her at Gabby's for a playdate. They were still being cautious about public appearances until Lucy was better about accidentally flaming things and Gabby was better about not shifting in public.

Teething. Toilet training. Toddlers were trouble even before they were shifting shape and breathing fire. The twos were going to be more terrible than ever.

It was quiet when he got to the tree, and Ian wondered belatedly what the protocol was for calling on Isadora. Cherry had said with exasperation that she didn't have a phone and there was no way to contact her, the woman just showed up where she wanted to be and it was very challenging to schedule around.

He listened to the wind in the tall trees and let his

senses relax. The smoke was clearing, and there were no active fires in his range. The air smelled like trees and grass again.

She's here, his dragon warned.

Ian turned to find Isadora behind him, dressed in clothing straight out of the sixties, covered in flowers, with flowing wide pant legs. A rainbow headband held her gray hair back. He wondered if she did that on purpose, materializing behind a person to catch them off balance, radically changing her appearance every time.

"I know what I am now," Ian said. "At least some of it."

She was silent and he had to flail on through the conversation without help.

"I'm an elemental. Like you. Only I'm a fire elemental, not an earth elemental. And I have a lot of questions."

She laughed at that, but Ian didn't think it sounded unkind. She seemed considerably more relaxed than the last time they'd met. Was it because the nearby fires were out? Or because Ian himself was not so much of an unwitting powder keg now?

"I'm not an *earth* elemental," Isadora explained patiently. "Rocks and dirt? No. I'm a life elemental. Plants and growing things are my domain, as fire is yours."

"How many kinds of elemental are there?" Ian wanted to know. "Are there a lot of us?"

"There used to be," Isadora said sadly. "But although we are long-lived, we are not invulnerable."

"My father died in a car accident."

"I didn't know him," Isadora said dismissively. She walked past him to her tree and put a hand to the bark. Her branches spanned overhead like a great cathedral roof. "He was half human, I would guess, since you are more diluted yet." She turned and shot Ian an appraising look. "You wouldn't be so powerful without the dragon inside of you. It is a dangerous combination, your abilities and his great strength. It's not a good fit. You don't match."

Ian's dragon was pleased by the assessment of his strength, but dismayed by the rest of Isadora's statement. Ian could feel him swirling in distress.

"I want to learn to control my power," Ian said firmly. "So I can teach my daughter how to control hers."

Everything about Isadora softened. "I have a daughter, too."

"Oette," Ian remembered.

"You young things are very confusing," Isadora confessed. "She is half human. If you will teach her about being human, I will teach you what I can about being an elemental. You do not appear to be *completely* idiotic."

Ian decided to take that as a compliment. "I'm not sure I'm the best person to teach her about being human, but I will gladly try," he said formally.

"I will return Adoette to Cherry's place of care," Isadora said decisively. "We will arrange for a periodic exchange of children and you will come here each fifth evening so I can assess your skills and direct your study."

Ian tried to figure out where fifth evenings would fall on The Schedule, then decided it didn't matter. He could change The Schedule if he needed to.

"I can do that."

Isadora vanished without further niceties and after waiting a moment to see if she reappeared, Ian gave the tree a polite nod and retreated down the trail.

He felt deeply relieved. He knew his path forward from here, and for the first time in a long time, had faith in his own abilities. But the feedback feeling hadn't gone away, and his dragon felt...mournful.

What's wrong? he asked.

You don't need me anymore.

Ian came to a stop so suddenly that he nearly fell over. *What do you mean?*

His dragon heaved a sigh and Ian had a sense of settling wings. *I thought I knew my purpose here, with you, helping you. But you have harnessed your own power, in ways that I never could, and you will only grow more skilled. I find that I feel adrift, unnecessary. The tree said that we were a poor fit. Perhaps...we do not belong together.*

You would leave me? Ian felt as if the gravel path under his feet had fallen away. What would he be without his dragon? *Who* would he be?

Parents thrust their fledglings from the nest, his dragon pointed out. *They do not cling to them forever.*

We could be partners, Ian protested. *Yes, you were like a parent, but we're more like equals than ever now. I...don't want to lose you.* The idea of life without his dragon shook him. *You saved me.*

Ian had an impression of an arching neck, humility in every scale of its body. *Instinct told me you needed me. It doesn't now.*

What does instinct tell you? Ian closed his eyes, trying to make sense of it himself. It was drawing him home to Lucy, and to Olivia.

Lucy, his dragon sighed. Then, with even more longing, *Olivia.*

Had instinct been calling them *both* to Olivia?

Olivia.

She had always wanted to be a part of something magic.

She didn't seem jealous, exactly, but Ian could see the longing in her eyes, and he remembered the wistful way she'd spoken of wanting to be a shifter herself. He knew suddenly that his happiness was with her...and that her happiness was with his dragon, and that he could never keep them apart.

I would not go far, his dragon said, and it was full of the same yearning that Ian had seen in Olivia's face.

Ian swallowed. It was terrifying and perfect: his mate, a dragon. He would have only his own magic in his head again. *You should go to her,* he agreed. *If she agrees to it. If she wants you.*

Who would not want me? his dragon demanded in a blaze of its usual self-confidence.

CHAPTER 38

Olivia hopped over the yellow road gate less gracefully than Ian had, and wished that she'd thought to wear rubber boots when she landed in a puddle. Her sneakers squelched.

"Isadora could have picked a better day for this," she complained.

"Isadora likes the rain," Ian said. "But we're not here to see her." He was being weirdly nervous and withdrawn again, and Olivia had to remind herself firmly that she wasn't being excluded and left out of his secrets, and that if she was, he must have good reasons. She trusted Ian. She loved him, and she was confident that he loved her too. He claimed that he had a surprise for her. A *good* surprise, he said.

It better be a *good* surprise. It was drizzling, her hair was sticking to her face, and Olivia had a hundred and thirteen science quizzes left to grade, so she was trying very hard not to feel impatient and cross about being dragged out into the forest.

"Then why are we here?" she wanted to know. "Isn't this something we could do somewhere dry?"

"You aren't going to want to do this inside," Ian told her.

Olivia was wild with curiosity. "Do *what?*"

But all he would say was, "You'll see. Probably."

"Here," Ian finally said, as they walked into the parking lot. He was visibly agitated, and his wet hair stuck up in all directions.

"Why *here?*"

"There's space," Ian said. "You can't see it from the road, and no one will come down here. Isadora's okay with us doing it here."

"Doing *what?*" As much as she loved Ian, Olivia was about ready to strangle him.

"There's something I've kept from you," Ian said.

Olivia's heart dropped to her stomach. Had she been wrong to trust him? Was this something more about magic that she wasn't allowed to know?

As if he guessed her turmoil, Ian stepped close to her and took her by the shoulders. "It's...good, I promise. But it's really big."

"*How* big?"

"Dragon big."

Olivia was completely lost.

Ian sucked in a deep breath. "Do you want to be a dragon?"

Olivia felt less lost herself now and more like *Ian* had lost his mind. Was this a practical joke? "I don't get it."

"Do you want to be a dragon?" Ian asked more earnestly. "I told it that you had to choose, that you get to decide. Yes, I know, she's the one, instinct says. But she *decides.*"

Olivia thought that the last two sentences hadn't been

aimed at her and her brain caught up with what Ian was suggesting.

"Your dragon…?"

"Could be your dragon."

Olivia might have fallen over backwards if Ian hadn't been holding her shoulders; she felt like the world had suddenly tilted in an unexpected direction.

"A dragon…" she murmured. She could be a real part of that magical shifter world that she was standing at the edges of. She could be something more than she was, something greater than she'd ever imagined. She could jump feet first into the enchanted waters, fly straight up into the air.

She might actually *fly*.

Ian was looking at her face in concern. "You don't have to be. The two of us have a good balance now and are making it work, you can say no, it's not like you'd be leaving it homeless or anything."

"Why on earth would I say no?" Olivia demanded. "Unless…are you sure? What about *you*?"

Ian's mouth curved up in a lopsided grin. "There are downsides," he warned. "It's a bossy dragon, and some-times it's hard to hold two conversations at once. Instinct takes some getting used to. The water in your shower will never feel hot enough."

"I want to be a dragon," Olivia said, bouncing on her feet.

"It's a challenging shift form," Ian added, even though he was grinning broadly now. "You have to be careful about where you do it, and stay out of sight when you do."

"I want to be a *dragon*!" Olivia repeated firmly.

"If you're sure…?"

Now he was just teasing her. "Ian!" she protested.

Then he drew her into his arms and kissed her.

Ian's kisses were always amazing, they never failed to leave her breathless and excited and full of heat. But this time, his kiss came with a blaze that started in her lips and filled her whole body. The rain sizzled off of her as she seemed to light on fire.

Olivia! Olivia! My Olivia!

There was a dragon in her soul, singing in joy, and she was whole and complete and she would never be alone again. It was alien and comforting all at once, and she felt powerful and gentle and utterly free.

She could shift, and as soon as she thought of it, she did, Ian jumping back out of her way as her clothing shredded off of her gleaming new form.

Oops, she thought in chagrin.

Was this why Ian had warned her to dress casually? Shifting her clothing with her was going to be a bit of a learning curve, and she suspected that she would find it even more challenging than the students at Tiny Paws did.

I will help you, her dragon promised. *We will learn together.*

Olivia? This was a new voice, but strangely familiar.

Ian?

He felt like home. Something was humming in her heart, like a favorite song that she could never tire of, like a smell that would always make her feel safe. *Is this instinct?*

How can I hear you? Ian asked in wonder.

His dragon—*her* dragon—answered them both. *You will always be a part of each other now*, it said in satisfaction. *You cannot live with a dragon so long and not take some imprint of it on your soul. And you are made for each other, as much as Olivia was made for me.*

Olivia shifted back into human form and shivered as the rain hit her bare flesh. Ian stripped off his damp flannel shirt and wrapped it chivalrously around her, but she didn't feel cold, exactly, only shocked. *I'm a dragon*, she said in his mind, full of wonder and joy. *I'm a dragon! What can I do as a dragon?* She could fly now, and shift, and shoot flames, perhaps?

Her dragon affirmed that, and it felt as full of elation and love as she was.

But there was one thing that she wanted to do first...and she was already mostly undressed anyway.

Olivia! Ian said in her head as she threw her arms around his neck and drew him down to kiss her. *I love you!*

The best thing about being able to speak in each other's minds now was that she didn't have to stop kissing him to tell him to take his clothes off.

Gravel is uncomfortable, Ian protested.

When Olivia might have argued, the fire inside of her at a new magical pitch, he swiftly added, *The station wagon seat goes down...*

They had to stop kissing to run hand-in-hand back to the car, where Ian demonstrated exactly how fast the station wagon seat could be put down, and then he was stripping off his clothing to crawl with her into the back.

"Olivia..." he said, just as she was about to kiss him into silence again. "I don't want to hurt..."

Olivia realized that she was smelling singed fabric.

You can't hurt us, his dragon—*her* dragon—reminded him, and that was all that mattered as they scrambled desperately for each other at last.

As hot as the lodge weekend had been, this was literally hotter. Olivia felt like a sun, hungry and wild for his touch. His skin on hers was the most exquisite sensation she'd ever felt, and then he was slipping his cock into her and proving that there were heights she hadn't known to aspire to.

He completed her, raised her to a fever pitch, and released her, and it was the most amazing thing in her existence when she felt his own liberation in her mind, their orgasms twining together like musical themes.

Afterwards, they lay together in the scorched station wagon, laughing in relief and touching and caressing each other.

"Do you miss it?" Olivia had to ask, humming in physical satisfaction and magical bliss. She was a dragon. She felt like her soul was too big for her body, like she was more than she'd ever known she could be. But could she live with her own happiness if she'd robbed Ian of a fundamental joy…?

His mindvoice burned with truth—Olivia didn't think that he could lie with it if he tried. *This is what was meant to be. I was living like I had radios tuned to different channels in each ear and now I'm just me and I have everything I ever wanted. More than I ever **knew** to want.*

I love you, she replied, with just as much truth.

He kissed her, slow and cooler now, but Olivia was confident that they could have gone again. From somewhere on the floor of the car, his phone alarm went off.

Ian groaned. "I have to pick up Lucy."

"Did you think you might get distracted?" Olivia asked with a giggle, remembering their first date. Sensible was still sexy.

"Honestly, I hoped I might," Ian admitted. "Though I had expected you to want to do more with flying and flaming than this."

"Is that a complaint?" she teased him.

"I promise it isn't."

They crawled out of the station wagon. "Your car is kind of a wreck," Olivia observed. "And I have no clothes." There were charred remains of his shirt, but it didn't really cover a lot. She mourned the loss of her bra; that had been a particular favorite and finding a good fit was challenging.

"I brought you a change," Ian said, pointing to a bag in the front seat. "I had to guess on the size, but I figured your first shift might be a little rough." He fingered the holes burnt in his own clothing. "I didn't expect this. I guess my dragon did more to keep me in check than either of us really realized."

Sensible was really, *really* sexy, and it also beat showing up naked at Cherry's to collect Lucy.

"We've both got a bit of a learning curve ahead of us, I think," Olivia said, drawing on the sweatpants he'd bought for her. Her dragon—her *dragon!*—was purring in the back of her head, starting to drowse and Olivia thought she knew a little about Seltzer's most boneless contentment at that moment.

Ian was waiting for her with a kiss when she got the T-shirt over her head. *I look forward to a lot of practice together,* he said suggestively.

CHAPTER 39

Lucy ran ahead of Ian down the hallway, shrieking and giggling.

"Fingers and feet!" Ian reminded her. "Fingers and feet!" He repeated it as he caught her up in both hands and tossed her up to catch and tickle her. "I got you! I got you!"

She howled in laughter, but carefully kept her human form, and Ian only faintly smelled smoke from her. "Good girl," he praised her, turning her tickles into cuddles. "Look how smart you are."

"Finners an feep," Lucy agreed. They had been working diligently on self control, and if Ian sometimes felt like he was training a puppy with sweets and hugs instead of dog treats, it was still remarkably effective. "No fie. No fie."

She wrapped her little arms around his neck and snuggled into him.

The hard times were always worth it for these moments of sheer happiness and love.

Ian's phone rang and he slung Lucy over to one side

as he dug it out of a pocket, expecting a call from the other half of his heart. His hope chilled at the sight of Wanda's contact information, but he sighed and swiped to answer.

"Ian," he said shortly.

"Hello," Wanda said brightly. "I was just calling to check in on Lucy."

"She's doing great," Ian said sincerely. He tickled her so that Wanda could hear her giggle. "And I'm glad you called, because I wanted to talk to you about The Schedule."

Wanda was quiet for a moment. "What about it?" she asked warily. Usually she was the one bringing up The Schedule.

"I've been keeping Lucy a lot more than you have and I'd like you to pay some of her day care expenses if that's going to continue," Ian said.

"Mummy!" Lucy hollered, reaching for the phone. "Mummy!"

"Patience," Ian told her. "Count to six!"

She couldn't remember what came after three, so that usually distracted her for a while. "Two, five, one, two…"

Wanda used that time to find a reply. "Well, she doesn't really need day care if you're home…"

"I work, Wanda," Ian said firmly. "This isn't negotiable and I've already talked to some legal counsel." Roderick counted as legal counsel, didn't he? "Of course, you could just take some extra days instead."

He wasn't surprised when Wanda didn't argue. "I'll pay half of it," she said briefly. "No reason to get lawyers involved." She probably didn't want to have to take care of a fire-breathing toddler for any more days than she absolutely had to.

"I'll send you a copy of this month's bill," Ian said. "I

already paid it, so you can pay next month's in full. Here's Lucy!"

He heard Wanda sputter as he handed the phone to Lucy. "Hold tight to the phone," he reminded her. And in a whisper, "No fire."

"Tree, five, six!" Lucy sang into the phone.

That had gone considerably smoother than he expected, and he'd gotten everything he needed. With Wanda paying half, he could afford to keep doing day care and get out from behind on his writing commitments and bills.

Ian was getting more perfect control of his own fire power now, too, though he usually waited until Lucy was sleeping or at day care to experiment, not wanting to set a poor example if he was sometimes sloppy with the flames he made. Isadora had given him several helpful tips, and the rest they were learning together.

Lucy handed him the phone.

"All done with Mommy?"

"Ah done!"

Ian made sure that it was hung up and turned off and started to put the phone in his pocket just as it rang again.

This call was from Olivia's number and it didn't matter how many times she called him, Ian thought that his heart would never not leap up in anticipation when he saw her contact information.

"Ian's loveshack. Can I make you a reservation?"

"Hi, Ian," Addison's voice said, thick with amusement.

Ian froze in mortification. "Hi...Addison?"

"Olivia's driving but asked me to call and let you know that we were running a little bit late. We found a great couch, but had to drive to Marion to get it."

Lucy was trying to grab the phone. "Not for you, sweetie," Ian said. "Oh, no! Sorry, Addison, that was to

Lucy! Sorry!" He facepalmed and Lucy copied him, nearly sticking her fingers in her eyes. "No worries about getting back late, we're holding down the fort and I'll be around to help unload the couch when you get here."

"Thanks, sweetie," Addison teased, and Ian could hear Olivia laughing in the background. "How's the book going?"

"Great," Ian said sincerely. Lucy stared at her hand and moved to picking her nose. "Yuck!" he told her. "That was for Lucy again," he clarified for Addison. "The book is actually finished. I'm doing a polish pass before I send it off to my editor, but I think it's actually a real whole grown-up book."

"Congratulations!" Addison said sincerely. "That must be really exciting!"

"It feels pretty tremendous," Ian agreed.

"Are you going to keep Lucy at Tiny Paws?" she wanted to know.

Ian thought about having the house to himself, about not having to worry about Lucy flooding the bathroom or setting something on fire. "There will be revisions, soon enough," he said. "And it's supposed to be a trilogy. Maybe I can write the next one in less than two years."

"Oh good," Addison said warmly. "We'd miss having her there."

Lucy seemed to have figured out that it was Addison on the other end of the line and she leaned close to the phone and Ian's face. "Addy, babba Sezzer floober! No fie! No fie!"

Addison laughed. "Good job, Lucy! No fire! We'll see you in about an hour."

"Bye, bye!" Lucy said enthusiastically. "Bye, bye!" She continued to say that for a little while and Ian put her down to run off some of her lingering energy. If he could get her tired out before Olivia got back, maybe he could get a good long nap out of her and he and Olivia could take her new couch for a test drive with their facing windows open so he could hear if Lucy woke up. He suddenly wondered if a baby monitor would reach that far.

Lucy ran the length of the house for the back door, then turned into a squirrel so she could parkour off the walls and make another lap of the house before she returned to Ian's arms.

"You took all your clothes with you!" Ian said, too proud of the feat to scold her for shifting. They were inside and alone, and he'd always tried to be very clear that safe shifting was okay. He didn't want her to feel bad or ashamed about her abilities, just to have some good sense and clear boundaries about when to use them. He wasn't sure if she would have any of the same problems being both a squirrel shifter and an elemental that he'd had as a dragon and an elemental, but he wryly realized that he was very uniquely suited to helping her through any problems that it might cause.

Nothing happened without a reason. Maybe his whole childhood ordeal was simply so that he had the tools to be the very best dad to the very best little girl.

Lucy tired of her hug and squirmed down again. "Sezzer?" she suggested. "Can we go play with Sezzer?" Sometimes she managed perfectly clear conversation, and sometimes she spoke absolute nonsense with exactly the same authority.

"Sezzer—er, *Seltzer*—is probably sleeping," Ian said. He had a key to Olivia's house now, and she had one to his, but he didn't feel entitled to go in without a better reason than to play with her cat. "Let's go in the back and play golf!"

Games with Lucy had taken on new joy now that he

had some regular respite from her. As much as he adored her, non-stop Lucy was a lot to handle.

"Goff!" Lucy agreed cheerfully. "Goff!"

She bolted out in front of him, reaching up to open the back door. "Birfday!" she remembered. "Birfday goff."

Ian came to stop in the back door. "Oh crap," he remembered. "I still have to plan your birthday party!"

"Crap! Crap! Crap!" Lucy crowed.

EPILOGUE

Tiny Paws was full of balloons when Olivia arrived. A few helium orbs were bobbing along with their weights, and more breath-filled balloons were scattered all over the floor.

It was more crowded than a day of day care usually was, because it was most of the day care kids and also a half a dozen parents were wiggling their stocking feet in the rug with their kids. It was strange to see them past the gate; very few of them wanted to take off their shoes every day when one of the day care staff was perfectly happy to usher their kids to the front and meet them there.

Adoette was even there, Isadora hovering in a corner with a watchful eye as her daughter wandered among the other children, clinging to her sapling pot and occasionally jerking it out of someone's reach with a possessive, "Mine!"

A handwritten banner over the animal cages proclaimed: "Happy Birthday Lucy!" with a judicious number of 2s in various colors with googly eyes and dancing legs. Olivia guessed that the numbers were Roderick's work—he was often drafted into drawing things for the day care.

"Two! Two! Two!" Lucy was singing, spinning around in her long princess dress in the center of the balloons. "I'm two!"

Gil was crying while his mother patiently reminded him, "We can't have cake until the candles are blown out. It's Lucy's birthday, not yours."

Olivia put her present for Lucy down on the gift table —it was a cat fascinator of her very own, because she always wanted to take Seltzer's home with her. She hoped it wasn't too weird to give a two-year-old squirrel shifter a cat toy, but really, *weird* was the new normal.

I'm not weird, her dragon protested.

Olivia was realizing that it had a very different relationship with her than it had shared with Ian. *You're not weird*, she promised. *You just take getting used to.*

And it was worth every learning curve. She was a dragon and it was every bit as amazing and fulfilling as she'd ever imagined it could be. She loved flying, she loved the swirl of instinct, and it was helpful knowing which of the naked middle schoolers were prank victims and which ones were careless shifters.

"Owiveh!" Gabby, a toddler just younger than Lucy, charged through the balloons for Olivia, who intercepted her and swung her up into the air. "Owiveh, aba dowalla!"

Olivia had even less luck understanding Gabby than she did Lucy, but she nodded sagely anyway. "Are you excited for Lucy's birthday?" she asked, bouncing Gabby.

"Oocy!" Gabby agreed. "Aggabada oo ah." She struggled to get down and Olivia bent and released her just before she shifted into four legs. The little girl took most of her clothing with her, but forgot her socks, so Olivia stooped to pick them up and tuck them into her pocket so she could return them to Roderick or Addison later.

"Are those socks in your pocket or are you just happy to see me?" Ian wanted to know, sweeping up from behind her to give her an embrace and kiss her on the neck.

"I'm always happy to see you," Olivia said, turning in his arms. "The socks are just a special bonus."

He kissed her properly then, and Olivia felt like her entire body was in a weird juxtaposition where everything was exactly perfect the way that it was…and wanting much, much more.

"Want to ditch this lame party and go have awkward car sex?" she suggested quietly. "Pretty sure we won't burn it out this time."

Ian laughed. "I think we might be missed," he said regretfully. "I'm here with the guest of honor. Besides, this is a great party. I made the banner myself. Well, some of it. And I blew up all the balloons. Well some of them."

"It really is a beautiful party," Olivia agreed, surveying it with him. The parents were trying to coax healthy snacks into the sugar-focused kids before the cake came out, and the excitement level in the room was at an all-time high.

Lucy was too enthralled with her princess dress to change into a squirrel, but she seemed to move no less fast, a red-headed blur through the room. (She had resisted the red-haired mermaid costume and insisted on the blue ice princess dress.)

"How's middle school?" Addison asked, with an upside-down owl in her arms. Olivia remembered Gabby's socks in her pocket and handed them over. Addison was wearing a rainbow vest with generous pockets that absorbed them easily.

"Middle school is definitely different than day care," Olivia laughed. "No dirty diapers or mystery messes. But there are a lot of hormones and tears and 'Documenting our research is too haaaaaard, Miss Lopez' and 'You give too much homework!' Only one fire in the lab so far."

"Amy coughed up her first owl pellet this week," Addison said wryly. "Top that."

They grinned at each other fondly. Olivia loved her job, but her short stint at Tiny Paws had rewarded her with a lifetime of memories and a dear new friend.

Ian and Roderick tried in vain to organize actual games, but the kids were too wound up to listen or follow rules, so they eventually just gave up and let them play. Lucy and Gabby raced in circles around the balloon-strewn room on two legs and four with Amy chasing them and squawking in outrage when she was left behind. Tara, who was much older than any of them, was reading quietly in a corner while her mother nursed her baby brother in the rocking chair.

When the chaos threatened to reach a new pitch, Ian sensibly called for cake and presents, which got everyone's attention in very short order.

"Cake!" Gil cried happily. "Presents!"

"Mine!" Lucy said ferociously. "They're mine!"

"Abababababa!" Gabby added.

Amy just shrieked.

Ian vanished into the back room to reappear with the cake, bearing two candles on it. Olivia knew that he hadn't needed a lighter to ignite them. He had solid control of his powers now and had even put the batteries back into his fire alarms.

Addison started everyone singing the birthday song, raggedly and out of tune, but not lacking in enthusiasm.

"Happy birthday, dear Lucy!" Olivia sang along with them.

Everyone clapped and cheered at the end of the song.

"Blow out the candles!" Addison encouraged.

"Make a wish!" Roderick reminded her.

Lucy pointed at the candles and they both went obediently out. "No fie."

That shocked and silenced her adult audience, but the children didn't seem to think it was at all out of the ordinary and after a pause, everyone started clapping again.

Olivia was standing close enough to Ian to hear Cherry say quietly to him. "We haven't talked about your hazard fee, yet."

"I'm sure it will be worth it," Ian replied with a sheepish smile. He stepped forward to cut the cake and distribute plates to all the children and any adults who wanted a piece. Olivia handed out forks and napkins, knowing that she'd be collecting them up afterwards from the bookshelves and play tables.

After cake came presents, as swiftly as Lucy could be prodded through them. There were washable markers and crayons, squirrel slippers with fluffy tails, books, packs of colored paper, and a microphone that sang a dozen popular children's songs that Olivia knew Ian was already sick of. She hoped the batteries were removable.

Her cat fascinator was received with the same enthusiasm as everything else, and Ian laughed knowingly at it. It would be a wand and a fishing rod and an object of great imagination adventures, Olivia thought.

The party broke up quickly after that, children growing tired and cranky as they realized that the parts of the party they'd looked most forward to were over and there were no forthcoming wonders. Olivia tried to convince Lucy to hand out party favors and finally did so herself. The children satisfied themselves with their consolation prizes and eyed Lucy's pile of loot enviously.

Harried parents thanked Ian and Lucy and tried to get their wound-up children to make polite thank yous.

"Ank ooo!" Gabby sang, wearing her new plastic sunglasses and waving a bubble wand. Several of the miniature bottles were already empty, some of them used and some of them spilled. Amy had tried to drink hers.

Finally, it was only Ian, Olivia, Addison, and Roderick, picking up the leftover paper plates and cups. Olivia felt like it was comforting, going through the cleanup routine she'd done with Addison for her job at Tiny Paws. Monk's work, she thought, the ritual familiar and fulfilling. Lucy and Gabby played in parallel, basically ignoring each other in favor of their new treasures. Both of them looked on the brink of falling over in place, and were starting to get shrill in their demands for attention from the remaining grown-ups.

"I miss this," Olivia confessed to Addison while Ian and Roderick took out the trash bags and cleaned the bathrooms.

"You miss the diapers and tantrums?" Addison teased, but her look was knowing.

"I honestly do," Olivia laughed. "I'm not going to break my contract with the district, but if you guys ever need some temporary help again over summer break, or on a holiday…"

"You are always welcome here," Cherry said warmly, coming from the back office. "And I'm not just saying that because you're a warm body."

"It's because you're a warm body with a brain," Addison teased. "We have pretty high standards here at Tiny Paws!"

Olivia was touched. "Thank you," she said sincerely. It felt like she belonged here. Even though she hadn't been a shifter like they were, they'd been warm and inclusive, trusting her with their children and their secrets without hesitation. And now, she was, and it was everything she'd ever dreamed.

Of course I am, her dragon said smugly.

"Thank you for letting us rent the day care for the party," Ian said sincerely to Cherry. "I didn't realize how far in advance you had to book the bouncy house and I was really in a bind. Lucy, we have to leave your presents in the bag so we can take them all home. Please stop taking them out."

Lucy squawked her protest as Ian picked up a toy she had abandoned due to space in her hand, immediately switching the object of her interest to the thing that was being put away.

"It worked out really well," Roderick said, scooping up Gabby as she whimpered in frustration at her own toy and rubbed her eyes. "A nice, familiar place for the kids where it was safe for them to shift. We'd love to do Gabby's party here in a few months."

"Just don't tell Veronica," Cherry warned. "I'm pretty sure this technically counts as a sublet and she'd try to charge me more."

They all shared grumbles about Veronica and finished cleaning.

They left the room clean and tidy, even knowing that Monday would see the swift destruction of their order, and went out the front door, testing the lock behind them.

"Thank you for coming," Ian told Roderick and Addison. Gabby was already asleep on Roderick's shoulder.

Lucy was still wound up and Olivia whispered "Fingers and feet!" to remind her not to squirm out of Ian's arms and shift into a squirrel while they were out on the public street. They were a block off of the busiest area of downtown, but there were a few people out looking for obscure shopping treasure in the antique stores and thrift shops that lined the neighborhood. The little girl kicked her legs and sighed in frustration.

"It was a great party," Addison said. "Thanks for having us. Give me a call, Olivia. We'll meet for lunch some weekend. Maybe hit a garage sale and see if we can find anything to top that two-buck wine decanter."

Olivia promised to stay in touch and walked back to Ian's car with a full heart. It was completely natural to get Lucy tucked into her carseat while Ian stashed the leftover party treats in the back. Most of the burned fabric had been replaced.

"Owivay," Lucy said sleepily, as Olivia buckled her in and checked the connections. She reached out one hand and patted Olivia lovingly on the cheek, as she often did with Ian. "Daddy and Owivay. Ah good."

All good, her dragon—*her dragon!*—agreed.

And it really was.

~

A NOTE FROM ELVA

Thank you for picking up Dragon's Instinct! I had such a wonderful time writing about Olivia and Ian, and I was cackling over Lucy's antics and all the juicy plot twists. I hope that you enjoyed it even a fraction as much as I enjoyed writing it. Read on for a sneak preview of the next installment, Unicorn's Instinct…

I would very much appreciate your reviews on Amazon, Goodreads, or Bookbub (follow me at any of the above) if you enjoyed this book! I love to hear from readers, and you are welcome to email me at elvaherself@ elvabirch.com with any questions, or if you catch any stray typos…or if you just want to say hi.

To find out about new releases, you can follow me on Amazon, subscribe to my newsletter, or like me on Facebook. You are also welcome to join my Reader's Retreat on Facebook for sneak previews, cut scenes, giveaways, and more—including the book I'm not writing!

I also write under other pen names—keep reading for information about my other available titles!

~Elva

MORE BY ELVA BIRCH

Want some more extra short stories, including a Shifting Sands Resort ménage? Join my mailing list for sneak previews, extras, bonus stories, and more, or join my Reader's Retreat on Facebook!

The Royal Dragons of Alaska: A fascinating alternate world where Alaska is ruled by secret dragon shifters. Adventure, romance, and humor! Reluctant royalty, relentless enemies…dogs, camping, and magic! Start with The Dragon Prince of Alaska.

Lawn Ornament Shifters: The series that was only supposed to be a joke, this is a collection of short, ridiculous romances featuring unusual shifters, myths, and magic. Cross-your-legs funny and full of heart! Start with The Flamingo's Fated Mate!

Suddenly Shifters: A hilarious series of novellas, serials, and shorts set in the small town of Anders Canyon, where something (in the water?) is making ordinary citizens turn into shifters. Start with Something in the Water! Also available in audio!

Birch Hearts: An enchanting collection of short stories and novellas. Unconstrained by theme or setting, each short read has romance, magic, and heart, with a satisfying conclusion. And always, the impossible and irresistible. Start with a sampler plate in Prompted 2 for fourteen pieces of sweet-to-sizzling flash fiction, or the novella, Better Half. Breakup is a free story!

A Day Care for Shifters: A hot new full-length series about adorable shifter kids and their struggling single parents in a town full of mystery and surprise. Start the series with Wolf's Instinct, when Addison comes to Nickel City to take a job at a very special day care and finds a family to belong to. Funny and full of feeling, this is a gentle ice-cream-straight-from-the-container escape. Sweet and sizzling!

Green Valley Shifters: A sweet, small town series with single dads, secret shifters, sweet kids, and spinsters. Low-peril and steamy! Standalone books where you can revisit your favorite characters - this series is also complete with six books! Start with Dancing Bearfoot! This series crosses over with **Virtue Shifters**, which starts with Timber Wolf.

BEHIND THE SCENES

What is Patreon?

Patreon is a site where readers and fans can support creators with monthly subscriptions.

At my Patreon, I have tiers with early rough drafts of my books, flash fiction, coloring pages, signed and sketched paperbacks, exclusive swag, original artwork, photographs…and so much more! Every month is a little different, and there is a price for every budget. Patreon allows me to do projects that aren't very commercial and makes my income stream a little less unpredictable. It also gives me a place to connect with my fans!

Come find out what's going on behind the scenes and keep me creating at Patreon! patreon.com/ellenmillion

UNICORN'S INSTINCT - SNEAK PREVIEW!

"Tara, are you done eating?" Vivian asked, hopping in on one foot as she tried to pull on her shoe and finger-comb her hair at the same time. Shane had wanted to nurse much longer than usual that morning, and mornings were already made of tight scheduling and too many things to do for the time that she had. She wasn't sure she'd gotten all of the conditioner rinsed out of her hair during her stolen two-minute shower. "We have to go, I can't be late!"

If they left in the next five minutes, it would give them ten minutes to get to the day care, she had to plan on five minutes there to get Tara and Shane checked in, if she could find a parking space close, then she had to get the paperwork for the insurance company notarized at the bank before her shift at the clinic. The bank opened at ten, her shift started at ten-thirty. If she could be there when they opened, if she caught all the traffic lights right, she ought to be able to just make it...

"Tara, where are you? You've barely touched your breakfast, why aren't you eating it?"

Tara's kirin head popped up from underneath her

chair and Shane, strapped into his high chair, cackled in glee. Tara tipped her deer- and dragon-like head and her whiskers trailed after her.

Vivian gave a little squeak of surprise. She had still not gotten used to Tara's new level of comfort with her shift form. Even though she'd known about them for a few years now, shifters as a whole were still a bit of a shock. "Tara, honey, not at the breakfast table! I know you're the kirin who could, but could you *not* right now?"

As swift as thought, Tara was a little girl again, remorseful and guilty. "I dropped my egg," she explained, holding a tiny piece of fried egg aloft. "Sorry, Mommy."

"I know you are," Vivian said, reining back her frustration with effort. Tara was at a sensitive age where she took everything really personally. "Let's eat as much as we can a quick as possible," she said encouragingly. "I'll get Shane ready."

Shane was just starting his adventures in solid food and he was gumming on his rice teething cake with drooly interest but he hadn't eaten much of it. "Can I have that for a minute, Baby? Just for a minute? I'll give it back."

Shane stared at her with uncertain eyes. Vivian tried to distract him and slip the cracker-shaped food from his fist. He grabbed it harder and began to cry. "Alright, we'll strap you both in," Vivian said, giving up on her plan to keep the cake from disintegrating in the car seat with him.

Still convinced she was going to steal his precious food and possibly that she was instituting some form of elaborate torture, Shane fought against being buckled into the car seat with considerable strength for his age and cried in protest. Vivian kissed his forehead and smoothed his jumper underneath the straps. "Someday, you'll forgive me for all the terrible torment I put you through. I hope."

He cried disconsolately.

Tara hadn't eaten anything else in the time that Vivian had gotten Shane ready and she was achingly aware of the hands of the clock above the sink, tapping steadily to *too-late* in the morning.

"We're just going to have to take it to go," Vivian said, sweeping it all into a zip-shut baggy. Tara protested because she hated to have her food mixed up in one bag, which is when Vivian realized that she hadn't packed a lunch for her daughter yet. A frantic search of the kitchen turned up a hastily-peeled carrot, a single-serve yogurt, and a three-pack of cookies. "I am the worst mother in the history of the world," Vivian muttered under her breath, rifling through the drawer for a plastic spoon.

Unfortunately, Tara heard her. "You're not worst, Mommy!" the little girl hastened to assure her and Vivian was not going to rush a big hug, even if she wasn't sure whose comfort it was really for when she knelt down to get it.

Shane's crying changed in tenor and Tara ran to find him a selection of his favorite stuffies to distract him while Vivian finished packing what passed for a lunch.

"We're going to get a puppy," Tara was telling Shane comfortingly. "It's going to be a yellow puppy with floppy ears."

"We're not getting a puppy," Vivian told her daughter with a sigh. "I don't have time to take care of a puppy."

Time seemed to be her constant theme, and not enough of it.

There was still a chance to make it on time as she finished getting everything together…

But there were no parking spaces in front of the day care, or for two blocks in either direction. Vivian finally pulled up tight into half a spot, the back of her car almost blocking a fire hydrant, and herded Tara down the street with Shane in the car seat over one arm cutting off her circulation.

Tiny Paws Day Care looked unassuming from the street, with its old Saloon sign above the door. Vivian was buzzed in and Teacher Addy cheerfully met her to take Shane while Vivian coaxed Tara to take her shoes off a little more quickly, please.

In a stroke of mercy, there was no ticket on her windshield when she finally got back to the car, but all of the delays meant that she had no time before her shift at the clinic to stop at the bank with her paperwork. As it was, she was scrambling in the back door about five minutes late, thinking regretfully of mornings in the past when she could breeze in ten minutes early to enjoy a leisurely cup of coffee and gossip with Crystal before getting started on the day's work.

"I'm here, I'm here," Vivian said, pausing at the sink to give her hands the fastest sanitizing wash in the history of the world. Did the birthday song still count if you sang it in your head at double speed?

Crystal reached around her to grab a clipboard hanging on the wall. "The new temporary pediatrician's assistant is here, and whew, boy, am if you are not ready to date yet, I am going to ditch my family and have myself a wild affair because he is *ready to ride.*" She fanned herself with the clipboard suggestively.

Vivian had to stare at Crystal in surprise and a little horror. Crystal was absolutely not going to risk her family for a fling with the new PA, but what really drew Vivian up short was— "Date? I can't date."

Jin had only been gone for a year and his death had left her with a pile of bills and a heart full of grief, pregnant and trying to raise a three-year-old daughter who could change into a Chinese unicorn. She was lucky enough now to have access to a day care that was designed to handle shifter children and generous about irregular payments, but it didn't feel much like luck the way she scrambled endlessly between her job and trying to be a mother, never getting enough sleep, working desperately to make her time and money stretch further than it ought to.

She didn't have anything *left* for dating. "Help yourself to the hot new guy," she said with a regretful sigh. "I've got my hands too full with the kids."

She couldn't tell Crystal about the shifting part, of course. Shifters were a well-kept secret, and keeping that secret was one of the many weights on her shoulders. What if someone found out about Tara and tried to take her away? Was Shane going to be a shifter? Jin said that shifters recognized each other, but Vivian was only human, so she had to assume everyone was a risk.

"He's a *pediatrician's* assistant," Crystal reminded her. "He'll understand about kids. Sarah says he's filthy rich but he drives a hybrid because he's totally into the environment, and he's apparently an amazing cook, too. He brought homemade cookies because it's his first day. Oh, and he volunteers with the fire service during the summers!"

"He sounds like a unicorn," Vivian said, even knowing that Crystal wouldn't understand the depth of the irony. Jin had been an *actual* unicorn, something he'd kept close to his chest until Tara had been born. Vivian waited for the pang of grief that inevitably came from thinking about him, but she must be more tired than she realized because it was only the faintest of pains. She was also starving; she had never grabbed breakfast for herself that morning, trying to get food into the kids. "Cookies, you said?"

"In the break room," Crystal said. "Oh, it looks like we've got the Thompson triplets coming in today. I wonder what body parts they've broken now. Talk about a trial by fire. Your unicorn is going to have his hands full with his first patients."

"He's not my unicorn," Vivian said sharply, but Crystal was gone.

She didn't want to faint taking the vitals of her very first patients of the day, so Vivian headed for the break room. She might have a dollar in her purse to get an over-priced stick of salty beef jerky or a bag of chips from the vending machine.

She smelled the cookies even before she got into the break room, chocolate and cinnamon. Crystal had said that the new guy brought cookies, but she hadn't said that it was a giant platter with six different kinds of decadent fresh cookies: chocolate chip, chocolate crinkles, cinnamon snickerdoodles, gingerbread, oatmeal raisin, and— thoughtfully in a separate basket in case of allergies— peanut butter. Vivian looked longingly at the sweeter choices and opted for one of the protein-packed peanut butter cookies. Probably two would be alright. Three might look greedy, even if she was breastfeeding.

She biting into her second, trying to savor it instead of wolf it down frantically, with her eyes closed, when someone behind her cleared their throat.

The cookie snapped in half in her hand and Vivian had to scramble to catch both halves, knowing that she looked ridiculous and clumsy as she turned and nearly choked on what she had in her mouth.

Crystal hadn't been kidding.

The new pediatrics assistant was absolutely gorgeous. *Ready to ride,* she'd said, and Vivian could see why. The guy was a page straight out of GQ, with dark hair, a beauti-fully-groomed beard, and a perfect, white-toothed grin.

"Good cookies," Vivian managed to say when she

figured out how to swallow again. She hadn't reacted to anyone like this since...she balked at finishing the thought. He looked like a movie star. The one who did Sherlock Holmes and superheroes. He was also wearing a smock that was covered in tiny teddy bears in top hats.

"I'm glad you like them," he said, and even his voice was perfect, with the tiniest touch of a Boston accent. "Instinct told me I should bring them in today…"

Continue in Unicorn's Instinct!